KA

ŽIŽKOV

Olšany Cemetery

VINOHRADY

VRŠOVICE

PRAGUE. I SEE A CITY...

PRAGUE
I SEE A CITY...

by
DANIELA HODROVÁ

translated from the Czech by
DAVID SHORT

JANTAR PUBLISHING 2015

First published in London, Great Britain in 2011 by
Jantar Publishing Ltd.
www.jantarpublishing.com

French edition first published in Paris in 1991 as Visite privée: Prague
Czech edition first published in Prague in 1992 as Město vidím…

This edition first published by Jantar Publishing Ltd. in 2015

Daniela Hodrová
Prague. I see a city…
All rights reserved

A CIP catalogue record for this book is available from the British Library.
ISBN 978-0-9568890-6-5

Printed and bound in the Czech Republic by EUROPRINT a.s.

CONTENTS

Daniela Hodrová's City of the Threshold

Daniela Hodrová, born in Prague in 1946, is perhaps the most
distinctive and sophisticated literary voice to emerge in Czech
literature since the fall of Communism. The text of *Prague. I
see a city...* was originally commissioned for a French series of
alternative guidebooks which sought to introduce European
cities through the artistic gaze of another. It was first published
in French translation in 1991 as *Visite privée: Prague*, together with
photographs by Anne Garde, a map and advice on where to stay
and eat and what to see.* It was published in Czech in 1992 as
Město vidím... (I see a city...),† the title taken from Alois Jirásek's
version of Libuše's legendary prophecy: 'I see a city whose glory
will touch the stars.' Hodrová's text thus took on a second life
as her fourth novel, in order of writing, a conscious addition
to the tradition of Prague literary texts by, for example, Karel
Hynek Mácha, Jakub Arbes, Gustav Meyrink and Franz Kafka,
who present the city as a hostile living creature or a labyrinthine
place of magic and mystery in which the individual human being
may easily get lost.

In *Prague. I see a city...* , Hodrová mentions all the legendary
and historical Prague figures and episodes likely to be familiar
to an educated tourist: 'Good King' Wenceslas, Charles IV, the

---

* See D.Hodrová, *Visite privée: Prague*, trans. C.Servant, Paris: Chêne, 1991.

† See D.Hodrová, *Město vidím...* , Prague: Euroslavica, 1992.

early church reformer Jan Hus, Rudolf II, the defenestration of 1618, Tomáš Masaryk, Karel Čapek, the German occupation, the Prague Spring and Warsaw Pact military intervention of 1968, the fall of Communism in November 1989, Václav Havel. Her aim is not, however, to provide a helpful narrative survey of Prague's history, but on the contrary to 'defamiliarize' Prague, in the words of the Russian Formalist Viktor Shklovsky, 'to impart the sensation of things as they are perceived and not as they are known'.* She also includes unusual, apparently symbolic sights – like the old woman pushing a doll in a pram – familiar to anyone living in Prague at the time of writing. Hodrová presents Prague's history not as a linear sequence of discrete personalities and events, but as a cycle in which everything is merely an unconscious repetition of something or someone that went before. Historical figures are not dead, but live on, imprisoned forever in the identity that historical, personal, literary or folk memory has given them. Hodrová describes Prague as a stage on which history is enacted and re-enacted, a city where the gap between fiction and reality, and between participants and observers, is as blurred as it was for Hodrová as a child sitting in the wings, between audience and stage, watching her father, the actor Zdeněk Hodr, perform.

Amid the chaos born of the abandonment of cause and effect, of ordered, linear history, and the collapse of conventional hierarchies of knowledge, the narrator of *Prague. I see a city...* senses other, hidden patterns that might be divined. Like all Hodrová's novels, *Prague. I see a city...* thus takes the form of a novel of quest, in which the heroine abandons the material world of everyday society and linear history, perceiving it as false, temporary and distracting, and journeys in search of her true identity. Prague becomes for Hodrová a counterpart to Theseus' labyrinth, Dante's Florentine Inferno, the allegorical city in Comenius' *The Labyrinth*

---

* V.Shklovsky, 'Art as Technique' [1917], trans. L.T.Lemon and M.J.Reis, in J.Rivkin, M.Ryan (eds), *Literary Theory: An Anthology*, Malden, MA, Oxford: Blackwell, 1998, p.16.

of the World and The Paradise of the Heart or, indeed, Wonderland in Lewis Carroll's novel. The contemporary reader-tourist is transformed from an unthinking consumer of manageable pieces of information that pander to preconceptions and simplify the unknown into his more ancient counterpart, the pilgrim, accompanying the author as she wanders through a strange and treacherous world, reading and re-reading the signs in search of the ultimate answer to Prague's and her own identity.

Hodrová enjoys an equally high reputation as a literary theorist, and in her studies of the novel of quest she describes how, in later twentieth-century examples, the hero frequently wanders in a world of text, striving in vain to attain knowledge not mediated by language. In Hodrová's novels, life exists in and is created by words alone. *Prague. I see a city...* begins by paraphrasing the first verse of John's Gospel: 'In the beginning was the Word, and the Word was with God, and the Word was God.' The Prague of *Prague. I see a city...* is a purely textual construction, brought into being by Libuše's prophecy and composed of all that has been said and written about it. Implicitly, for Hodrová, when the twelfth-century monk Cosmas playfully suggested in his chronicle that the city's name derived from the Slavonic word for 'threshold', he ordained that Prague would become ever after a 'city of torment' (the title of Hodrová's trilogy of novels preceding *Prague. I see a city...* , taken from the *Divine Comedy*), an intermediate space between death and redemption, where identities, times and stories converge. Hodrová consistently depicts a world woven from texts, a fallen hierarchy, in the ruins of which she both nonchalantly plays and anxiously seeks a way beyond. In *Prague. I see a city...* , the story of the Prague Golem, the man of clay allegedly fashioned by a sixteenth-century rabbi to protect the Jewish ghetto, exemplifies how historical fact is masked by legend and then by fictional reworking. The Golem is animated by a *shem*, or piece of parchment inscribed with magic words, and Hodrová fears similarly that she has awakened Prague, which she calls a monster, by writing about it.

In *Prague. I see a city…* , however, Prague has also been awakened by 'revolution'; the novel is suffused with the atmosphere of the year following the fall of the Communist regime. Hodrová notes that, when the regime fell, she stopped writing her third novel, *Théta* (Theta), lest it become a different text. Her trilogy, especially the first two parts, is permeated by an atmosphere of somnolence, consonant with the conventional characterization in Czech culture of the 1970s and 1980s, in which the dead are more alive than the living, and the non-conformist questing hero withdraws from contemporary society to escape this living death. In *Prague. I see a city…* , Hodrová seems inclined both to succumb to the post-November euphoria and to step back into the knowing, sceptical margins that have seen all this before, as she does more persuasively in her next novel, *Perunův den* (Perun's day, 1994), to which *Prague. I see a city…* looks forward. She celebrates the carnival atmosphere, in which everyone briefly embraced her conception of existence as dynamic and unstable, in a constant state of change, of death and re-birth. At the same time, however, she senses that the mood is passing; she sympathizes with the new president, the former dissident, Václav Havel, as others become disillusioned with him, but links him to previous disappointed men who wore the Bohemian crown, which, in her view, for Havel has become a new form of imprisonment. A new order is being enthroned, with the depressing commercialization of her city at its heart.

Hodrová's fiction provides a refreshingly unfamiliar perspective on post-war Czech literature, which has generally been read and judged abroad through the politicized prism of the Cold War. Hodrová belongs to that generation of Czech intellectuals who were just too young to participate significantly in the 1960s cultural liberalization in Czechoslovakia and had to pursue careers during the much more restrictive Normalization of the 1970s and 1980s. Hodrová was not associated with the dissident opposition to the Communist government in that period, working for a publisher before becoming a researcher at the Academy of Sciences in 1975.

However, through her work on medieval literature and the history of the novel, founded on a highly individual, inventive synthetic reading of twentieth-century theory and tracing the continuity between medieval and twentieth-century culture, aesthetics, psychology, theology and philosophy, she developed a subversive vision of literary creation wholly at odds with the world-views advocated by both regime and anti-regime ideologues. During the Normalization, she encountered problems when submitting her scholarly work for examination or publication, while her first two novels, dated as written between 1977 and 1984, were not sanctioned for publication until early 1989. Their appearance was then, however, further delayed by the fall of Communism, after which publishers prioritized previously unsanctioned literature.

In both her fiction and theoretical work, Hodrová stands apart from the mainstream, showing affinities with only a small number of Czech contemporaries, but aligning herself with a much longer Czech and European literary tradition. Her depiction of her mostly female central characters as incorrigibly curious, solitary, tenacious, mischievous, naive, inscrutable and plucky not only corresponds to a certain Czech literary self-image, but may also be read as an ironic self-characterization, as she effectively admits in *Théta*. Her fiction epitomizes the attempt in the early 1990s to free Czech literature from political interpretation and exploitation and to distinguish between those who try to insulate themselves from the chaotic uncertainty of existence through the imposition of a false order and those willing to take up a precarious position 'on the edge of chaos' (as she entitled her monumental poetics of the twentieth-century literary work).

Prague. I see a city… , with its insight into the atmosphere immediately following the fall of Communism in Czechoslovakia and seductive re-imagining of Prague and its history, is ultimately no more than an introduction to Hodrová's world-view. At the time of writing, Hodrová's major novels have yet to be translated into English. They present a great challenge to the translator because of the word-play that pervades and arguably structures them, though German and French translators, among others, have made valiant attempts to replicate her games. Like Prague itself, words in Hodrová are places of initiation which, crossed and re-crossed, disclose ever more meanings and connotations. The search for a final order becomes the infinite uncovering of hidden connections and patterns, the ever greater revelation of multiplicity and disorder. For Hodrová, the painful charm of human existence lies precisely in this hopeless yearning to be liberated from an experience of life as intermediate and incomplete, an experience incarnated in the 'city of the threshold' that is her home.

Rajendra A. Chitnis
Bristol, April 2011

FURTHER READING

Literature in post-communist Russia and Eastern Europe: the Russian, Czech and Slovak fiction of the Changes, 1988-98 / Rajendra A. Chitnis. RoutledgeCurzon, 2004.

Twenty-first-century Central and Eastern European writers / edited by Steven Serafin and Vasa D. Mihailovich. Detroit, Mich. : Gale, 2010.

'Spinning her web: Novels of Daniela Hodrová through a gendered lens', Elena Sokol in Rosalind Marsh (ed.), *New Women's Writing in Russia, Central and Eastern Europe*, Newcastle: Cambridge Scholars Publishing 2011.

When one day Prague shall standing die,
When not a living breath shall come
From man or any living beast.

KAREL HYNEK MÁCHA,
A Dream of Prague

But here, where errantly unreal we walk,
sleeping what we are, and suddenly to see the truth
at last in the dreams through which we roam,
it will be false, for we shall be dreaming.

FERNANDO PESSOA,
At the Grave of Christian Rosenkreutz

In the beginning, the city was, to me, a word – Prague. Somewhat later, lying on my back in my cot, I would watch strips of light flitter across the ceiling as a tram passed down the street. I imagined the city as a beast of prey sleeping somewhere far away (in my childhood it felt as if our house was on the outskirts, though in reality it was barely half an hour's walk from the centre). The beast's breath, hot and exotic, sometimes wafted in through the window, washed over me like a wave. But the beast in its den slept not, it was watching and waiting. For me to come?

Only later, after I left my cot with its metal bars (my head once got stuck between them – or did I read that somewhere?) and for the first time in my life went out onto the balcony (at the time I didn't know that some years before a Jewish girl had jumped from it rather than leave with the transport; nor did I anticipate that the sentence describing her downward flight from the fifth floor would stand at the very beginning of my first novel), did the word, which until then had been the name of a beast, change into the uncertain, alluring and disquieting space that opened up beneath me then on the balcony. Originally I thought the city was just that wide-open space, that dark depth, confined on four sides by a wall. The point being that the tenement block of my childhood stood directly opposite Prague's largest burial ground – Olšany Cemetery – and the window of my infant bedroom looked right onto it. At All Saints and other feasts the cemetery would change into an ocean-going liner, all a-twinkle with countless little lights. It would come in at the window, almost floating, like the ship in

Fellini's *Amarcord*.

If I am seeking to evoke that first ever perception of the city, it may be that I am doing so from a belief that the city rose from nothing in parallel to how *I* arrived in the world and came to an awareness of my own self. Before my birth, the space on which it sprang was still being folded geologically. And as the hands of my grandfather, the senior consultant Dr Jan Jerie, brought me into the world at Bubeneč sanatorium, the primordial sea that still filled the Prague Basin was overflowing, its bed ripped apart by erupting volcanoes. Solidifying lava formed the rocky projections overlooking St Procopius' Valley, the cliff at Vyšehrad and the Karlov bluff. The trilobites and other ancient animals discovered in the 1840s by the French geologist Joachim Barrande became fossilised in them. In those ancient times, which corresponded to the first years of my life in the first year after the war, the sea would still flood even the spot where, one day, during the Plague, the Olšany Cemetery would come into being, and lap at the house where we lived in a flat left behind by some Germans (in my bedroom there was still a puppet theatre of theirs, with a blue velvet curtain).

Then the sea began to recede. The cellar walls sparkled with salt crystals, which the concierge's son, Peter N., and I would try with our tongues. At the time, the house was still for me what the entire city became later – Hell, Purgatory and Paradise, or perhaps just an underworld, since the boundaries between the various spaces were less than clear (and isn't that one of the features that typify this city as a whole – this merging of places of mercy with places of perdition?).

And the sea continued its retreat. See, out of the dark depths of antiquity the River Vltava is emerging, and its tributaries that will create transverse valleys. And now the river is slowly descending from the heights of the ridges that outline the Prague Basin today, depositing the layers of sediment that will become Flora, Olšany, the plateau of Pankrác and Bohnice Hill. And finally it drops back to the level of Charles Square and Vodička

Street. And as I first stand upright in the wooden playpen in the middle of my room, hunters first appear in the Prague Basin to pursue wild animals in the forests, collect honey from the trunks of lindens and make sacrifices to demons at crossroads. They will be followed by the corded pottery people, then the archer people with their bell-shaped goblets. In the late fourth century BC the Celts will arrive, followed, around the start of the New Age, by the Marcomanns. And only after that will the Slavs appear. That will be when my hunchbacked nursemaid will take me out daily in my cream-coloured pram around the wall of Olšany Cemetery, never once managing to get me to sleep. They will worship their idols, Svantovit and Černoboh, and invoke their ancestors, their "holy forefathers". Sacred trees rustle above the flames that blaze over their funeral pyres. They dance around the fires in masks. The baby in the pram catches the smell of the reeking blood of sacrificial victims.

TABLEAUX VIVANTS

For me, the city has been a word, a beast in hiding, a gradually receding sea, the house where Peter N. would wait in the cellar. And it has also been the father who would bend over me in the night on his return from Vinohrady Theatre. His face used to smell of make-up and grease (the theatre smell had replaced the smell of exotic fruit the city used to exude when I was still a babe-in-arms). Ever since, the city has had for me some mysterious link with theatre; city and theatre are one, together constituting some hallowed scene – a *visio* – revealed after the curtain goes up. In my perception, the curtain of the playhouse-city is to be found somewhere near the National Museum, where the Horse Gate once stood. There, above the square dominated by the statue of St Wenceslas (how little does that mighty metal horseman resemble the pious youth of legend!). Before the eyes of the audience standing on the forestage in front of the museum, overlooking a

3

fountain that never plays, the curtain parts and *tableaux vivants* begin to file past. Come to think of it, the downward slope of the square also reminds one of a stage. Though it doesn't slope down in the ordinary way of theatres, towards the orchestra pit, but the other way, towards Můstek. Where classical theatre buildings would have the prompter's box, here, every May Day and for many a long year, they would erect a stand, which they would deck overnight in red fabric (fabric? – bunting more like). Here the speeches of presidents would ring out, the masses, marching past beneath the stand, would greet them cheering and clapping, which later tailed off somewhat, until this particular tableau was transferred to the foot of another rostrum – on Letná, which, from autumn onwards, would become home to a circus.

Wenceslas Square – scene of *tableaux vivants*. Some are merely presented, others have been genuinely played out.

Scene one: THE SLAVS ARRIVE IN BOHEMIA, an idyllic picture of the life of the Slavs of yore. They live in hill forts where the future city will be. Their prince in a crimson, gold-embroidered robe sits on his princely throne in a hall of columns. At Vyšehrad or on Opyš – where one day Prague Castle will stand.

Scene two: LIBUŠE'S PROPHECY. Princess Libuše (Libussa), having had Přemysl summoned away from his plough to take up the throne, puts the crimson robe on him, as the legend tells us. The princess is standing on the forestage of the Museum in her ritual gown and with a diadem on her head, looking for all the world like a Byzantine priestess. In her hand she has a sprig of linden. Her passionate eyes gaze out over and beyond the tunnel next to the Main Station. She prophesies: *I see a great city, its glory touches the stars.* That's what Cosmas, the medieval chronicler, writes (in Latin). In Smetana's opera *Libuše*, which the National Theatre puts on whenever there is something to celebrate, Libuše, surprisingly, does not prophesy the future city's glory. Having seen visions of several Bohemian rulers, the Hussites and, finally, King George of Poděbrady, she sings: *What next? Fog hides the view and conceals much from misted eyes, dreadful secrets – curses...*

4

The presidential box is occupied by Masaryk, then Beneš, then Gottwald, then Zápotocký, then Novotný, then Svoboda, then Husák, then Havel. And the princess sings on: *My dear Bohemian nation forever here shall dwell, and overcome in glory all the dread of hell.* And then the chorus joins in: *The nation of Bohemia forever here shall dwell, and overcome in glory all the dread of hell! Hurrah!* Only President Hácha, a puppet manipulated by the Germans during the Protectorate, never heard Libuše prophesy; the opera was banned at the time. But he might have heard it later in the yard of Pankrác prison as one crazed prisoner was led out into the sun. *The nation of Bohemia forever here shall dwell, … all the dread of hell.* The composer himself heard not one note of this aria, since by 1873, when he completed the opera, he was totally deaf. Shortly after Gottwald's death (the disease that killed him is still withheld from the public, as is that which killed the creator of the national opera), at the beginning of the 1950s dark age, secret service agents burst into Professor Haškovec's villa and emptied the jar containing the composer's brain down the lavatory. By mistake? Deliberately? I see a great city… It shall overcome in glory all the dread of hell! Hurrah!

THE MURDER OF SAINT WENCESLAS

I actually see two pictures before me. In one, a very young Wenceslas is having his hair cropped on the altar steps of the cathedral, as had been the custom in Slavonic and Teutonic princely families since pagan times. That ritual seems to contain the other picture within it – a scene of murder. Legend has it that beneath his princely apparel Wenceslas wore a horsehair shirt. He is said to have prepared the sacrament of the Body and Blood of Christ himself, he himself reaping the wheat with his loyal servant, himself threshing and grinding it and baking it into the Host, himself turning grapes into wine. But there the idyll of early Christianity in Bohemia does not end. The next picture opens with the murder of St Wenceslas' grandmother, Ludmilla, who had raised him. Two of her mother Drahomíra's men, Tunna and Gomon, are strangling Ludmilla with the veil they have torn from her head. Finally I see the scene of St Wenceslas' own murder. His brother Boleslav draws his sword, slashes, but is knocked to the ground by Wenceslas. Along come the men who will complete the murder. Three of them – Hněvsa, Tista (Časta) and Tira (Tyr). The picture holds one significant detail: as Wenceslas flees towards the church which might afford him refuge, one of the priests (his name unknown) closes the door against him. Then comes Boleslav's men's furious ride to the Prague court, Wenceslas' retainers are all killed, the children drowned in the Vltava, the women married off to other men, the priests and clerics of Wenceslas' churches robbed and driven into exile. This happens on Monday, 28 September, nine hundred and thirty-five in Stará Boleslav.

And then, three years later, Wenceslas' body is being conveyed to St Vitus' Cathedral. In secret, at night. Blood drips from the wound inflicted by his brother Boleslav. I can sense nearby the priest who had closed the door against him as he fled. He touches the relics, wrapped in a crimson shroud with white crosses, cautiously, as if they might burn him. He lays them in a tomb of gold, silver, precious stones and pearls. *Saint Wenceslas, Duke of Bohemia...* Later, three hundred years later, they will be touched by Charles IV. He will set the crown on the saint's whitened skull. The crown is decorated with twenty-one gemstones, the largest of the six sapphires round its circumference is cornflower-blue and is the third largest known sapphire in the world. Atop the crown sits a cross, with a fragment of the Crown of Thorns in its cavity. HIC EST SPINA DE CORONA DOMINI, the Latin inscription reads.

For centuries the crown, along with the imperial sceptre, orb, ring, vestments, sword and cross, has lain in the jewel chamber above the Chapel of St Wenceslas, which is approached by a secret spiral staircase and is protected by a door with seven locks. The crown only comes to life at coronations of the Kings of Bohemia, on whose heads it briefly sits. The last on which it sat, in 1836, was the oedematous head of Ferdinand V (the Good-Hearted), a sick king who ultimately turned into a puppet. *... come now and take up thine inheritance...* Several times over, however, the jewel chamber was empty for years at a time. First, when King Sigismund had the crown jewels conveyed secretly to Hungary. That is when the gold sheath of the St Wenceslas sword went missing. In 1867, when the crown jewels came back to Prague, the train, which deliberately crossed Moravia and Bohemia by night, was greeted by crowds at every station and accompanied by bonfires on every hilltop.

No, Ferdinand the Good-Hearted was not the last on whose head the crown sat. Nor was it Hitler, who could not find the hidden crown in March 1939, though the jewels' hiding-place was later revealed (the traitor's name is not known). On 19 November 1941, a tall man in polished boots mounted the spiral staircase to the jewel chamber. He couldn't resist and placed the crown on his head. *Saint Wenceslas, Du...* A strange image lodged in the mirror – a man in a dark uniform with a crown on his head. It was *Reichsprotektor* Reinhard Heydrich, who was assassinated twelve months later.

Ferdinand the Good-Hearted is sitting in his bath chair in the middle of the royal gardens. He makes to touch a place on his head, he has a feeling of having been pricked by a thorn, but he cannot raise his arm (but then how could he? It is the arm of a puppet). Ferdinand inspects his arm closely, for an hour, perhaps two. Then his gaze slips towards the ground, to a bed of red roses. The bed is in the shape of a five-pointed star, but Ferdinand doesn't find that strange (nor does it seem strange to President Havel, though it's more likely that he cannot see that far from his office window). The sound of quiet weeping comes up from somewhere, unless it's the singing of the nearby Belvedere fountain (one of the paintings on the summer house walls is of the Murder of St Wenceslas). *... May thy luminous brightness cast light upon us, dulled as we are by sin...*

My childhood years, played out in a house and inner court near Olšany Cemetery, are linked in my mind with the city's Middle Ages. My expeditions out of the courtyard, scene of our games, led at their furthest to two places: one was Hagibor, a vast, desolate open space close to the Jewish Cemetery in Vinohrady – a 'wasteland' that at one end merged into tennis courts (beyond them the edge of Strašnice, that borough with the spooky name [*strašit* is 'to frighten'], to the child's imagination a marshland with strange lights floating over it at night), and the other was Gallows Hill (Sibeniční vrch, or Šibeničák), which rose above the Olšany duck pond. It was probably from there, Gallows Hill, that I first spotted that famous panorama with the spires of St Vitus' Cathedral. In the nineteenth century it was also seen by a waiter, Fiala, the last man to be hanged here, before the hangman tugged at the noose – and perhaps for a moment longer too.

The Middle Ages are linked to a strong sense I have of the boundedness of space; a special meaning attaches to walls and ramparts – the wall round our yard and the wall round the cemetery. We would climb over the cemetery wall and hop onto the graves. Our fingers would sink into the damp soil after recent rain and come out smelling of mildew and wine (or was it the smell of the plague?). Twenty years later many of the graves would be desecrated by vandals; the ancient tombs of German families (we would try in vain to decipher their names carved in black-letter script) would be littered with faeces. One day I would even look into a cavernous interior, a heap of bones curled up in the corner of an open coffin. But for me in those days the cemetery was not a place of terror, perhaps because I had lived since birth in close proximity to it. I learned later that during the war a Jew had hidden in one of the tombs; my great-uncle would take him food. I don't know how that cemetery story ended; in the novel I put it in it ended badly. Mr Šípek the caretaker informed on them and both were then shot – Mr Turek and Mr Klečka, as I christened them in the novel. But the dead of the novel live on, nothing in it ends once and for all, everything that happens comes round again and again in one way or another. And how will it be in the present text? It could be called 'the living memory of places' – each place is a playhouse of the scenes that have taken place and continue to take place there. Sometimes, these images in a place's memory get mixed up, popping up either simultaneously or out of order. In all likelihood, that's what it will be like here too. And in my novel there is also another principle at work – the way places imagine things. On the basis of their memory, places make up their own stories, surrounding themselves with events that have never occurred there, but could have. And the same applies to things (this text will be full of all manner of relics) – things not only have their actual stories, but also invent other stories for fun. All that's needed is to give in to their urge to weave plots.

One day, Peter N. and I were digging a hole in the corner of the yard behind an old silver spruce; I don't remember what for. In it we found two glass bull's-eye marbles and a shred of red cloth. The colour had largely gone out of it, but you could still tell the pattern – tiny, bright crosses. If we had continued digging, we would have found under the yard the grave of some hunched figure or a bell-shaped goblet. I expect we threw the scrap – probably a piece of clothing – away somewhere (we kept the marbles), having failed to recognise in it the remnant of a sacred shroud. One day, when I was well into adulthood, even on the threshold of old age, I would see that scrap of cloth in a museum. That, you see, is how places and things make up stories.

A GAME

The city's main landmark has always been its Gothic cathedral; its spires outlined above the river. In 1989 the site of the Jewish cemetery in Žižkov suddenly sprouted a television tower, rearing in all its grandeur above the tangle of rooftops. The cadaverously

9

white stalk of this gigantic stinkhorn (*Fallus impudicus*), as my husband nicknamed it (in folk-speak it has acquired numerous other disparaging names), it has become the city's new, phoney landmark. It casts its shadow on the Church of the Sacred Heart and the roof of the house where I have lived since the age of thirteen. Sometimes I feel it grew there overnight and one day will just decay and collapse. That day, though, isn't here yet. That autumn, the boom of a massive crane also popped up outside my window. An orange-coloured iron grab with two men in it moved slowly along the street, the men glanced into the room where I was writing one of the end chapters of my novel *Theta*. Their faces were expressionless. Down in the street knots of people gathered, watching the odd antics of the two men. To this day I don't know whether it was simple coincidence or whether it had something to do with the trial going on in the court building in the adjacent Jagellon Street. On trial was Václav Havel.

That autumn I was disquieted by one other phenomenon. Rumour was rife that somewhere outside the city, in Hrdlořezy, special squads in red berets had built a second Wenceslas Square, complete with Mezibranská, Ve Smečkách, Vodičkova and other tributary streets, also the National Museum building. They had even raised a statue of St Wenceslas on that square. It was said to be only rough-hewn and the saint unhorsed. And he was no longer accompanied by our patron saints Cyril and Methodius. Day after day in Hrdlořezy they play the St Wenceslas game, as I've called it. This is how it's played: a wall of shield-bearers guards the statue; whoever breaks through the wall, hoping to become St Wenceslas, gets a whipping. Reality had begun to duplicate itself in a strange way (or had I not noticed this duplication earlier?).

And other strange things would happen. In the courtyard of the Strahov Monastery, which houses the National Literary Archive with its famous library, and also the Literature Institute where I work, a Bohemian lion suddenly appeared one day, the model for a statue, hidden for years from the public gaze. Unlike the lion that rests pacifically in the bend of Chotek Road, which winds up to the Castle (that lion was originally intended for the Royal Baths as Ischl, but the monarch was put off it as a reminder of the arms of the Kingdom of Bohemia), the Strahov lion is rampant – it's a lion roaring. For months on end the lion, which had sprung up out of the nation's oblivion and non-existence, stood at ground level in a corner of the courtyard; foreign tourists would lie down beneath its body and take photos of its huge leonine sexual organ, and then one day, without ceremony, it was craned up onto a pedestal of battered ashlars. The appearance of the lion, for all it became an object of merriment, seemed to bode something positive.

WORDS

In the real city, something was at work which those who played the St Wenceslas game in Hrdlořezy and later, on key anniversaries – 21 August and 28 October – in the real Wenceslas Square, hadn't reckoned on – the magic of words. In his *Experimental Psychology*, Břetislav Kafka writes of the separate envelope around the Earth made up of the feelings, thoughts, memories of all people, living and long dead. And is there not a similar envelope round cities as well? And is it not made up of the fates of their numberless inhabitants, but also of all the myths and prophecies connected with the city and all the texts ever written about it, and even – if we admit the existence of black holes and time warps – those which have yet to be written about it? And it will also be, or actually already has been, joined by this text … A text about the theatre of the city which will be another variant on the *città dolente*, city of torment, theme.

That is what Dante calls the underworld in his *Commedia*, but he doubtless also meant his native Florence, to which he could not return on pain of death. I haven't had to leave my native city, and yet it has been and is a torment to me. For me, descending into the city, a descent almost in the sense of a katabasis into initiation, is a descent into its past, but at the same time a descent towards my own self, my own identity. This is so in those three of my novels that are conjoined by the title *City of Torment*, and in this work too, which pertains to them, sharing their rootstock. Immediately prior to it I wrote my novel *Theta*. There, that Greek letter is not associated just with death, with the word *Thanatos* – death. But also with the proofreader's mark ϑ, which means *deleatur* – to be deleted. (By a curious chance, the typesetter of the first, French, version of this text inserted, instead of ϑ, some non-existent letter, as if he had taken fright at the sinister power of this character.) In the novel I found a substitute victim for myself – Eliška Beránková. I had this character pass through the massacre of January 19, 1989, the anniversary of Jan Palach's death. People dragged her, covered in blood, into the Church of Our Lady of the Snows (this really happened to one woman, but I don't know her name). Inside the church the lion from Strahov stepped onto her chest. In that scene in the novel the statue of the lion came alive, then gradually evolved into a symbol. The city evolved into a *lion city*.

After a time, I happened on the Czech translation of an extract from Libuše Moníková's novel *Pavane for a Dead Infanta*. In the underground passages beneath Prague, which here and there crisscross the lines of the metro, a princess (the very one who prophesied the city's star-reaching glory and whom I saw in Wenceslas Square in the form given her in Mašek's picture exhibited in the Musée d'Orsay in Paris) is watching a dying lion with a tumour on its head where the crown should be. I was struck by the similarity to the motif in my own novel. Where did this congruence between our texts come from – a text by one person who had left Prague twenty years earlier and a text by another who had lived there all that time – whence this motif of a lady and a lion? There is no other explanation than that it was *there* – in the envelope, or rather carapace of words and pictures, themes and stories which enfolds the city and us ever more tightly.

In recent years and months, the heraldic lion has been coming back to life in writings about Prague. They are permeated with long-buried, symbolic meanings associated with Czech statehood. But at the same time contrary forces have been at work – those that come out of the writing. It seems to me that texts have metamorphosed reality by the very fact of having been written. Even if they have remained shrouded in a foreign language, as in Moníková's *Pavane for a Dead Infanta*, or concealed in a desk drawer, like my own *Theta*. The words they contain are prophecies, which suddenly, as if overnight, begin to acquire sense and fulfilment. Not far from George of Poděbrady Square, where I live, is Škroup Square. It takes its name from the composer of the Czech national anthem, *Kde domov můj* – 'Where is my Home?' This circumstance (though perhaps not it alone) was the inspiration for the scene in *Theta* where a blind youth is singing the anthem in this small round square. His singing affords relief to the tormented souls crossing the square (to me too, as I daily pass this way in the guise of Eliška Beránková on my early evening trips to see my dying father in the hospital in Kubelík Street). And lo and behold, a few weeks after I had written this scene, without anyone having read it, a demonstration was held in the square and ended with the singing of *Kde domov můj*. So in the beginning was the word… words? Or was it that, in this case too, a word written down here and now, encompassed in print what had already been inscribed long ago somewhere up there in the envelope round the city (Kafka calls the envelope *protonation*)?

In the autumn of 1989, I continued writing *Theta*, the third and last part of the trilogy. In the text I gradually found more and more meanings of the Greek letter. It was no longer just the letter of death, exclusion (was I afraid that I too would be excluded, swept from the face of the city by that orange-painted grab, my manuscript destroyed, burnt on a bonfire – for fear of its power?), but also a letter of life. The point being that this letter also denotes a peculiar undulation that goes with the regeneration of the vital powers. Then in one scene in the novel, a mutation of the letter, like the one committed by the French typesetter, sprang into life in the margin of a manuscript being proofread by one of the novel's characters. It had changed into a scarab. The ancient-Egyptian hieroglyph in the form of this sacred beetle meant *to be* and also *memory*. Then Eliška Beránková, just like that letter, tried to step outside my manuscript, to change from a literary figure, manipulated like a marionette (in the novel, Prague is truly a city of marionettes), into a living person. At the same time she was seeking her wild beast; she had met it once before in childhood...

November came. As if overnight the city awoke from its mortal faint, from its semi-being and semi-consciousness. On November 17, at the place where, several months earlier, the blood of my character had seeped into the ground, real people bled. The city began to revive with words. Words covered shop windows, walls, the concourses and walkways of the metro, which until then had been a silent mausoleum to the ruling ideology. MIND THE DOORS. NEXT STOP LENINOVA. THIS TRAIN TERMINATES HERE. PLEASE LEAVE THE TRAIN. When, later, from one day to the next, the students washed all the graffiti away, deleting all those words at the behest of Letter Theta, I had my first moment of fear as I entered the metro. What if it had all been a dream – like the dream in Calderón where a prisoner dreams he's become king? Fortunately it wasn't a dream, or, if it was, at least we haven't woken up from it yet. A revolution of words, an almost fairground battle of words really did take place last year, though its tumult now reaches us only dimly. The city is once more slipping back into its sleep, its unconsciousness, its oblivion.

In those November days, something fundamental happened to the life of this city, to my life. I finished writing *Theta* at the very moment the battle broke out, for at that moment the city ceased, at least briefly, to be a city of torment. I found it impossible to continue with the novel; it would have changed into a different text – someone else's. Those words about the euphoria, about fusing with the jubilant crowd on Wenceslas Square, where I had also stood on the Wednesday of that decisive week, found me in a lie and had to be *deleata* from the manuscript. It was suddenly

clear that at the point where, in Dante's *Commedia*, the mounta
of Paradise is outlined above Hell and Purgatory, I couldn't f
low in the poet's footsteps. Or was I merely afraid of words th
might alter reality? And does that now not happen, do the words
I write no longer change the city back into a city of torment, a
playhouse-city in which they are performing an *auto sacramental*?

REQUIEM

Since November 1989, Národní třída (National Avenue) has metamorphosed into a church. At the site of the martyrdom, beneath
the arcade of the Kaňka house and that of the Metro Palace, candles blaze day and night, melting down into burning puddles of
wax. The church even has its high altar – by Platzer's statue of
St John Nepomucene outside the Ursuline Convent, which still
houses the Institute of Endocrinology. Relics of the martyrs still lie
at the foot of the statue – a brown shoe, a crumpled, red-checked
scarf, a bloody handkerchief. People squat down here and light
more candles, others bow their heads as they pass by, the odd
one kneels down. Maybe they're praying for the soul of Martin
Šmíd, the one who died and rose on the third day.

In the spirit of the dualism that prevails in this city, there
were two students of that name, but only one was in the 17th
November procession from Albertov, only one found himself
trapped in National Avenue, only one of them was to receive
a crown of thorns. Which one of the two was to be commem-
orated at the service in Charles Square? The crowd gathered at
the edge of the park were looked down on by the Jesuit saints
over the church portico, St Ignatius de Loyola also looked down
on them from the freshly gilded mandorla on the gable. A little
way off some policemen were kicking their heels. Once, long ago,
Charles IV had a wooden tower erected on this very spot; holy
days would witness, displayed within it, the relics of which he
was a passionate collector. These included a scrap from Pilate's

cape, two thorns from Christ's crown and several pieces of the sheet in which His body was wound after death (it might have left an imprint on it like on the Turin Shroud), and even the milk of the Virgin Mary was here, and the shoulder of St Anne… People might have been expecting the actor Haničinec, whom someone had lifted onto his shoulders, to display some relic of St Martin Šmíd, just as Charles IV, in his day, used to display the body of St Vitus, brought here from Pavia. Until then, Prague only had the arm of that divine young man, who was placed in a cauldron of fire. *He is the scent of incense, he has the cocks crow to signal that day has dawned, and he arises out of the last shades of night all in crimson…* "We've had reports," the actor Haničinec shouted in a voice made hoarse, "that the student Martin Šmíd is alive. The theatres are going on strike…" Now the crowd understood; there would be no memorial service, no sainted arm would be displayed this time, not yet. The crowd disperses, but with dark mutterings, a decision is coming to fruition inside them.

My husband and I turn into Barley (Ječná) Street. In the window of the Catholic charitable organisation there was a display of crimson vestments, vestments of the colour donned by a priest on Good Friday. He truly lives, truly?

CORPUS CHRISTI

In George of Poděbrady Square, under the mantle of night, rats fight over the leftovers brought to them by dear little old ladies. Perhaps the Rev. Slabý (whose name means 'weak') can also see them from his window, but rats are probably not close to his heart. Since his arrival on February 1, the Church of the Sacred Heart has been impressively lit by numerous floodlights, glowing deep into the night like an ocean-going liner sailing towards my window. Only the gigantic clock set in the tower refuses to go, in vain they repair it, and it persists in showing some ridiculous time; right now it is fixed at ten thirty-four, perhaps the time of

Father Slabý's eternity, the time of the rats, whose dark bodies scuttle about beneath the radiant church.

The rear end of a mobile games arcade – a bus with videogames, which has dropped anchor by the church, carries the legend JESUS. And it also has the face of Václav Havel, not torn down yet like the face of Josef Bartončík, agent Bartončík, only shreds of his are left on walls and lamp-posts, with holes gaping behind the lenses of his spectacles. Not even Václav Havel can see the rats, of which there are more and more in the square (there may also be more and more little old ladies, their hands ever more generous), he is hanging with his back to the view and is made of paper.

I suddenly hear music, it reminds me of the oompah-bands you get at village funerals. No, it isn't a funeral, it's a Corpus Christi procession. Striding at its head comes Father Slabý (no weakling he!) with the monstrance, behind him a retinue of girls and boys in white. I am watching the procession with the poet Emil Juliš, the one who wrote: *We come near the fire.* "A Corpus Christi procession, that's a first," I tell him. Then I remember the rats. I hope the procession doesn't run into them! Nothing happens, the procession moves solemnly on, the body of Christ borne along in front, I can't see it from the balcony, it's hidden from sight and so small.

After a while the square is deserted once more. I know that if I looked out I would see old women scuttling through the veil of darkness towards the Church of the Sacred Heart (one of them might even be the Blessed Zdislava, one-time Lady of Lemberg and Jablonné, her apron full of bread and a glass of pure water in her hand). With blissful smiles they broadcast sower-like their Corpus Christi crumbs.

TELEVIEWERS

REPENT! That's what it says on every lamppost. EACH ABSTEN-TION IS A VOTE FOR EVIL. In many places hangs the portrait of the man they have declared a traitor, in tatters, the president of the People's Party looks down on the city through hundreds of dark eye-sockets. Repent! An old lady on the ground floor of a house in Laub Street opens a window every night and calls: "In now!" Who's she lost? – has her child died, her dog strayed, a hideous mongrel? She's mad. In another street, not far from the house of the Čapek brothers, another old lady leans out of a mezzanine window and asks me – in Polish: "What's the time?" Is she also mad? "Four minutes after half past ten," I reply. She seems not to have understood properly, but nods and smiles blissfully like the old Jewish lady in *The Shop on Main Street*. I hurry down the street, perhaps afraid another old lady might lean out of her window and address me in a language I won't understand, and ask me a question to which I won't know the answer. Only later, as I approach my home (snagged as ever by the claw of the TV tower), do I realise, glancing at the church clock, that it still isn't going, that I told the old lady the time by it, the time of eternity in which the city is frozen. Could I also be mad?

As I passed Václav Havel's portrait on the back of the bus with videogames I was suddenly struck by something odd. What if everything's different? Is the man we think of as king (after all, the people would gladly set the crown of St Wenceslas on his head and he would then bow on all sides with jerky movements, a bit reminiscent of Ferdinand the Good-Hearted, that marionette-king), not actually a prisoner (I can often read the anxiety in his eyes as he steals a glance at his guards) and are we not merely watching a television drama, a soap-opera about the Velvet Revolution? As the seasons – winter – spring – summer – autumn – pass across the paper face of King Václav, our latter-day Wenceslas, the anxiety of the prisoner grows ever more apparent. I wonder, when will this bus with videogames, stuck here since Christmas like a fish in shallows, leave? It will take away with it this picture of Václav Havel, imprinted on its back like the face of the Saviour on Veronica's veil – a *vera ikon*, an image of a prisoner-king. The play will end, the curtain above the Museum, where once the Horse

Gate stood, but also, a little way off, the Arena, will slowly fall, wound down by invisible stage-managers. Then next morning we will get on a metro train, hear the voice of an invisible guard (the guide to the Underworld?) announce: MOSKEVSKÁ. MIND THE DOORS. But they've renamed this station, haven't they? At every revolution names are first in line; yesterday, this one was still called ANGEL (after Angel House, which they knocked down to make way for the underground railway) ... And suddenly we'll learn that VYŠEHRAD is GOTTWALDOVA again. And so it is with all other names, valid only for the duration of the play being performed in the City of Torment. And if we could glance at the face imprinted on the bus with videogames as it drives away from the city we would see that anxiety and anguish have changed it beyond recognition. And shortly, after a few more seasons have passed and the bus has called at a few more places, it too will be in tatters – like the face of that traitor (or was he too a traitor only in the play?) – a *vera ikon*.

AT THE MUSEUM

When I finally extricate myself from the underground labyrinth, from the confusion of newspaper-sellers and people scurrying to the station (it's Friday afternoon) and come up the escalator, I see before me the neo-Renaissance building of the City of Prague Municipal Museum. PRAGUE, ORPHAN QUEEN ... It towers over the arterial road, between Florenc bus station and the de-molished Těšnov railway station, like a castle on a desert island. I still have to weave my way through the Gipsy kids playing on the steps outside the museum entrance.

Inside an old woman sits knitting. Guarding the entrance to the City's memory. I'm reminded of the one who admitted Conrad's Marlow as he made his way into *the heart of darkness*. Might not knitting, like spinning, have some esoteric meaning? Might it not symbolise the structure and motion of the world, the motion of

Creation? And is it not also a symbol of Fate? Moira, who might just be creating the world or knitting the fate of this city, condescends to let me in. I avoid her eyes. Inside I find two more. Not knitting, sitting with their hands in their lap. ... BEAUTY-RICH, HIGH IN REGARD AND CURSE-LADEN... In the medieval section there's no one. On one wall, under glass, I examine a scrap of the shroud in which they wound that man murdered on the cathedral steps, with its white crosses on a crimson field. My attention is caught by two heads. The head of Pomona from Krocín's fountain that once stood in Old Town Square (Pomona's chin and nose have been disfigured, but no one has touched the apples in her hair), and the giant head known as Bradáč ('Beardy'). Its purpose is still a mystery. When that head, projecting from the wall of Charles' Bridge, is under water, it means that Old Town Square is flooded. But the Museum Bradáč has been hung so high that if it were under water, it would mean that the entire city was flooded, only the hills and the church-spires, and the television tower, would project above the water. ... GREAT IN COMBAT, GREATER YET IN BONDAGE BY THY PRIDE...

On the next floor up they've got Langweil's model of Prague, I walk all round it, admiring the work's perfection. All that's missing is for this miniature city with all its churches and houses to be peopled with puppets. The impression is an odd one, of a city without people, like after an outbreak of plague. I meet no one here either.

I hadn't known that the Museum was then hosting an exhibition: PRAGUE 1968. I entered the room not quite at ease. I thought I was alone, but then I noticed an old man standing next to a panel with the inscription VICTIMS OF AUGUST and struggling to read some yellowed newspaper. Then I ran across a boy, about eleven. He was scuttling silently among the panels, as if he were running about the maze on Petřín Hill, and he seemed to be looking for something.

...THE JUSTICE OF HISTORY PLUCKS THE FLOWERS OF PEACE TRIUMPHANT WITH WHICH TO ADORN THY

BROW (an inscription in the Museum). The Moiras had by now sat down together. As I pass them, they happen to be discussing the Gipsy kids outside the door. At the top of the steps I pass the Wheel of Fortune. Wheel of Fortune? – Mánes' astronomical clock, its roundels illustrating the cycle of the seasons and the sequence of the farmer's year, glitters in gold. The impression is of a mask, though this clock could actually be real, perhaps because there is no motion behind it and it does not show any time.

The Gipsy children are no longer playing on the steps. I looked back one last time before I leave this island of memory and descend underground. Neither the old man nor the boy has come out of the museum yet. The water is rising.

PUPPETS

At the Castle, the last King of Bohemia, Ferdinand the Good-Hearted, turned into a puppet, one of those miraculous automata that used to be shown in Prague in the nineteenth century. The one-time king would sit in his coach, always conveyed by the same route from the Castle down Spur (now Neruda) Street, across Radecki (now Malostranské) Square, across Charles' Bridge to Ferdinand (now National) Avenue – he particularly liked that street because it bore his name – and thence to Stromovka Park and back. In the early days, the King would still alight from his coach, walk along the street bearing his name, take up a position on the embankment and, staring absently down onto the river, he would sit awhile on a bench by the Ursuline convent, right next to the statue of St John Nepomucene, where, one day, the relics of students would be displayed. And he would give the time of day to passers-by – turning round this way and that and raising his hat in a regular rhythm even if at a given moment no one had greeted him, the former king, the last to have had the crown of St Wenceslas on his head. In those days Bedřich Smetana would come every Friday and play for him – the *Miners' Chorus* and *Spirit of the Mountains*, which Ferdinand liked best. And then the now puppet-king, living out all those long years at the Castle, stopped alighting from his coach, but he kept turning his head left and right and raising his hat. And then even that motion ceased; the puppet's mechanism must have broken down.

The king, metamorphosed into a motionless puppet, would sit in his Bath chair and look at his toy – a miniature Swiss chalet. He would stare at the chalet with the same absent gaze as he would stare down across the City when his chamberlain pushed him up to the window. The City would become Langweil's model of Prague, which is exhibited in the Municipal Museum. The puppet would imagine walking along the embankment and doffing his hat. He would enter the Swiss chalet in the middle of the Castle and doff his hat, or rather crown, a tiny miniature crown, the kind they sell with an equally tiny sceptre and imperial orb in jewellers' shops. Then the King, suddenly just big enough to enter the Swiss chalet in the Castle and don the miniature crown, would feel the crown slip from his bald head, roll down Spur Street, across Radecki Square to Charles' Bridge. There the puppet would lose sight of it, since his eyes are not those of an eagle and the crown is so very tiny. Later the puppet just sits in its Bath chair (driven out of the Swiss chalet on the grounds that a toy costing 100 florins is wasted on it) and gazes absently at the spot where the cottage had stood and into the abyss where the City had stood.

The story of Ferdinand the Good-Hearted, who took the twenty-six years he spent at the Castle between his abdication and death to change into a puppet, seems to me to be a prime example of a phenomenon that has been at the back of my mind for some time. The Castle (or the whole City?) is afflicted with a particular curse: anyone who stays there long enough gradually turns into a puppet. Didn't the same thing happen to Emperor Rudolf, who ultimately hid himself away from the world and the light? And didn't President Husák finally change into a puppet, looking out from his armchair by the window down onto Langweil's model of Prague, until they took his toy away? And mightn't President Havel go the same way if he decided to move from the embankment to the Castle? Some of his gestures already have the jerkiness of puppets, but his eyes are still alive, very much alive, roving anxiously. And the City beneath his gaze is also still alive, not having changed yet into Langweil's model. But for how long...?

AN IMAGE IN AGATE

"This is my face," exclaimed the poet. Over there by the bronze door with the ring hanging from it that Wenceslas held on to as they murdered him. It's his portrait, the Jew can't deceive him as he tries in vain to persuade him that it's the face of Napoleon. Hadn't he pointed it out deliberately and wasn't he now relishing his horror? Where did his portrait come from, the portrait of a madman – in the agate that lines the walls of the St Wenceslas Chapel inside St Vitus' Cathedral, in this alien city? There has just been a glimpse of the Jew's long cape close by one magnificent silver tombstone, whose radiance made his ermine-white hair flash. "Wait, Laquedem!" He hurries after him, wanting to get out. He is as white as a sheet, desperate at having seen himself as a madman, so afraid that he might one day go mad. And he may also be afraid of all the things he might yet see here. And he's right to. After all, this is where the hero of Meyrink's novel *The Golem*, in his preoccupation, will swap hats with the long-dead Athanias Pernath (a hat in the shape of a prostrate eight, the sign of infinity, which has a tarot *pagato* on its crown) and will then have to live a life of misery. And here too K. will have to wait in vain for the Italian who is to guide him round Prague. Here K. will discover a pulpit previously unknown to him, with a miniature spiral staircase leading up to it (isn't miniaturisation one of the concomitant features of this City's demise?), looking more like the decoration on a column. A priest will mount the pulpit and tell him the parable of the doorkeeper and the man from the country.

"This is my face," the poet repeats outside the church. Laquedem the Jew smiles and says something about this being a city of faces, everyone would find his own in this chapel. And not just there, all you have to do is look: A strange city, the poet muses as he descends the Castle Steps. Ahead of him the Jew's brown cape flaps. The Jew holds on to his wide-brimmed hat so as not to lose it to the wind blowing from the Vltava below. Now they will descend into the City. During the night they will turn up in the ghetto. Laquedem will die there, but his death will be only apparent – for this is the eternally Wandering Jew.

I know I would also discover my own face in the St Wenceslas Chapel. Though this isn't possible; they recently closed the chapel to visitors and now you can only look in from across the rope by the bronze doors. From here I can't even see as far as Wenceslas' ring. Apollinaire's face and mine are enchanted there in stone. For eternity.

SHEM

I once dreamed that I was in the Prague ghetto. As is often the case with dreams, I knew it was a dream and that the ghetto didn't exist, and at the same time I felt that I had dreamed my way down to another dimension, lurking beneath everyday reality. The ghetto had sprung up in the city like a sparse fungus growth, thrusting up to the surface of the stage-set of Paris Avenue. The old houses with reeking butchers' shops and junkshops had previously been hidden behind the elegant Art Nouveau and eclecticist façades, which had parted like a curtain. It was as if someone had touched the shem of the Jewish Quarter, pronounced the magic formula and it had sprung to life like Rabbi Löw's clay Golem. And one day the Romanesque houses spellbound in the cellars of Gothic houses, and Gothic houses spellbound inside Baroque houses may also come thrusting to the surface.

Where is that shem? I read somewhere that it had been inserted under the tongues of the houses (in ghettos in particular and Jewish literature in general, the perception of houses as living organisms is the most natural thing in the world). For years I thought I knew about one shem. I was shown it by Jan E., a film director. The shem was outside the door of a house in Broad (Široká) Street, which runs up past the old Jewish Cemetery. He showed it me as a great secret that could be entrusted to one person only. The shem was roughly on a level with my head. Gently I touched the little oblong tablet underneath the cover. Nothing happened, but then I hadn't said the magic words.

But what if I *had* set off the mechanism of the lost City which announced itself even in my dream? At that very moment the tumbledown Jewish houses had just begun to grow imperceptibly out through the walls of turn-of-the-century houses. The ghetto, with its projections, nooks, dead-ends and narrow winding streets and passages, with its exotic smells, had begun to spread out from Broad Street (the main artery of the original Romanesque settlement out of which the ghetto had sprung in the Middle Ages, next to a ford) all the way to Maisel Street and Paris Avenue. And suddenly the streets had different names: here was Narrow (Úzká) Lane and Rabbi (Rabínská) Street, Sparrow (Vrabčí) Lane and One-End (Slepá) Street, Gipsy (Cikánská) Lane and also Red (Červená) Square, and the entire quarter was walled round. I saw Jews gathering in Red Square to pray in public at the time of the Black Death in 1770 (or am I myself back in that time of plague?). Exceptionally, the women knelt down next to the men, old men next to children, among them three fidgety little girls who kept standing up, their elder sister having great difficulty in making them kneel down again. Now they are beseeching the Supreme Being to restore their town to life. I watch to see if I could spot the rabbi among them, but Daniel Mayer wasn't there.

Paris Avenue, which leads from Old Town Square to the river Vltava (on the elevation right opposite it a gigantic statue of Stalin once towered, but for many years now there has been a gaping void, one day plays will be put on underground), is busy, crowds of tourists stream along it heading for the Square or the Intercontinental. Suddenly I see a knot of people. An old man is lying on the ground, his brown coat spread out around him like wings, his wide-brimmed hat placed by someone under his head. "He's dying," says someone leaning over the prone figure, and, since the man who had apparently been accompanying the old man (or the old man him?) does not understand, though he seems to guess the sense of the words, he says the same sentence in German and English and then in French: *Il va mourir*. And only now does he see that the stranger has understood him, that he has used his native tongue. And then this man who speaks so many languages opens his coat and rips his shirt lengthwise in an age-old ritual gesture.

So there it is. The Wandering Jew, who had been accompanying the poet, has died again, but his death is only apparent, just as the demise of the Jewish Quarter was only apparent. Today I know that that little tablet in Broad Street is just a *mezuzah*, as found on the doorposts of Jewish houses, not a magical shem. But how, then, can I explain … ?

AT THE CATHEDRAL

In the literature of Prague the Cathedral is a place of supernatural encounters, a place of apparitions. The heroes of neo-Romantic novels meet their doppelgangers in churches, they discover images of their faces there, like the French poet, *épouvanté* to descry his face *dessiné dans les agates de Saint-Vit*. A character in Meyrink's *Golem* swaps hats in St Vitus' with a stranger and then lives its owner's long past life. Here he will also hear the confession of a woman terrified at some mysterious intrigue. In the same cathedral, unidentified by name, but identifiable through certain details, a key scene in Kafka's *Trial* is played out. K. hears the preacher's Parable of a Man from the Country who spends a lifetime waiting outside his personally designated door to the Law. His problem stems from his failure to ask after the purpose of his existence. The Cathedral is the place where he might come closest to self-knowledge; in it he would find himself *within*, in the realm of revelation. But he fails to understand and does not enter, so he is condemned to wandering and to die on the edge of the City.

Suddenly the candles flare more brightly, the images over the altar come to life. In the background a door opens and a grand procession enters the Cathedral. Christ descends from the arms of the cross and strides towards the altar. Dressed in priestly vestments he serves Mass, raises the paten with the host and the chalice with the consecrated wine. Such a vision is vouchsafed to the hero with a *Gothic heart* in Jiří Karásek ze Lvovic's novel. Just a few years later – during the First World War – another Czech writer has a similar vision. Around Christmas. He enters the church, where a few people are at prayer. Suddenly the door of the St Wenceslas Chapel opens, enter a procession of priests with burning candles. They are singing: "Saint Wenceslas, Duke of Bohemia, our Prince, intercede for us with God, the Holy Spirit…" The Cathedral is dark, only the vestments and silvery bald heads of the old men gleam in the flickering flames of the candles. "Thou art heir to the Land of Bohemia, bethink thee of thy people… Grant us eternal life, and to those who shall come after!" They disappear into the sacristy, the Cathedral is bathed in darkness. He is still kneeling on the hard, numbingly cold stone floor. – Who? Karel Čapek.

Čapek published his memory of this experience in *Lidové noviny* on 18 December 1938. This article might be the source of the legend that the writer deliberately had himself locked in St Vitus' Cathedral in order to catch pneumonia and die. Whatever the case, the vision in the Cathedral, which included the St Wenceslas chorale, was the last time Čapek spoke, alive, to the nation in its time of torment. On 25 December 1938 he died of pneumonia. At the time, the National Theatre, out of fear, did not hang out a black flag and declined to lay out his mortal remains.

One other image came to my mind in connection with St

Vitus' Cathedral – that of its laying waste. This happened under the Hussites or later, in 1619. The Cathedral doors are gaping open into the night. Two men are casting down a wooden cross, the Saviour's body becomes detached from it and falls onto a pile of what were once paintings and statues. A dog runs inside, large and gaunt. It sniffs at some relics. They catch it and roll it over onto the cross. They nail it to it and raise it up. They shine a light on it. The dog's tail hangs down. It howls in dread.

AT THE CASTLE

Where, from the 1950s on, the presidium of the Central Committee of the Communist Party would meet, they would always erect a stage before New Year's Day. It was given over to Young Pioneers from all over the Republic. First, the President would watch a *tableau vivant*, for instance about war, peace and the new generation. One of the beings on stage, struck by an unseen projectile, was played on this occasion in 1960 by me. I remember sinking to my knees and protecting my head with my arms. Then we would come out of our death-dream, stand up, advance to the front of the stage and declaim in unison the sentence: "We are the generation that has germinated, Peter." The President's name, Antonín, would have made more sense, but I think this was a quotation from Julis Fučík, that hero executed by the Germans. (In St Pancras Prison [Pankrác] they could show tourists Fučík's cell. He would sit there at a little desk, a ream of paper before him, the title A REPORT WRITTEN ON THE SCAFFOLD written across the top sheet.) In the afternoon, tea would be served – cream rolls and cocoa. The President would walk among the Pioneers, from time to time awarding one (selected in advance?) the distinction of being asked a question – how he liked his cake, where did she come from. I remember that as he passed by me (I took a step back to let him pass) he fixed me with absent eyes.

I can see him sitting in the half-light of the auditorium, to his left the glinting reflection of the *trompe l'œil* windows, to his right windows looking out onto the Deer Fosse. He sits motionless, at the end of the performance he rises and claps, sparingly, crisply. The Hall is empty, he is alone. No, he isn't. Sitting with his back to him is a man dressed in black, which is probably why I didn't notice him. I go closer. Now I can see that his apparel is relieved by gold lace and a white ruff. The man is sitting in front of the statue of a kneeling youth. The youth has no arms, perhaps for having used them to protect his head from Apollo's dart, but in vain, a god's aim being always accurate. The man in Renaissance apparel is leaning to one side in his armchair and meditating over the torso. He has been meditating for many a long hour. The youth still has his head and member, but one day he will be cast, along with the other scraps left over from the imperial collection, into the Deer Fosse. Thereafter he will be headless, with a stump for his member. And eventually the youth, the youngest of Niobe's sons, will relocate from the Deer Fosse to the Museum of Sculpture in Munich, sold in 1782 for 10 kreutzer.

He is still sitting there with his back to the President, his eyes fixed on the statue, while a girl Pioneer recites a poem about the road to new tomorrows. And the reason he sits there for so long is that he is afraid to set forth from his art room to his bedroom. Who will protect him in those long corridors from Matthias and his men? The only ones he trusts are the stoker Markert and the Jew Kühbach, and lately not even them. Did not Mohamed roar just then? He doesn't even trust Laurentiana, she too knows Tycho de Brahe's prediction that the life of the lion is tied to the life of the Emperor by a magical bond.

As the Young Pioneers pass out into the adjacent hall, where cream rolls on paper plates and cocoa in paper cups are waiting for them, the man in black hauls himself out of his armchair. That *other* rises at the same time, no, not the President, the man in that same satin suit with the white ruff. Is it his image, or is he, Rudolf, on the contrary, the image of that *other*? Again he hears the lion roar. Beneath his cloak he touches the horn of the fabled unicorn

– he'd taken it with him – Ainkhürn is miraculous, perhaps it will protect him on his way through the labyrinth. Where is Markert, damned Mar...!

During the revolution of 8 May 1945, around nine in the evening, the radio reported that the Castle was on fire. Students from the Masaryk Halls of Residence in Dejvice ran to the scene, meaning to save the Castle with their bare hands. The Germans were burning their paperwork before leaving. They caught the students, pricked out their eyes, cut off their limbs and tossed them into the Deer Fosse. The torsos lay there for several days in a heap sprinkled with lime. The white bodies of Niobe's sons.

WENCESLAS SQUARE

According to the Prophesy of the Blind Boy, the knights sleeping inside the rock at Vyšehrad will wake up one day when Bohemia is in its direst straits, and come riding out with St Wenceslas at their head on a white horse (possibly the stallion Arda, the model for Myslbek's statue). And then, on the open space beneath the Horse Gate, a battle will be fought and blood will flow into the City and flood Wenceslas Square. Another version of the prophesy says that when the blood washes the first step of the memorial, the statue will come to life, St Wenceslas will brandish his sword in the direction of Blaník, the knights will ride out and go into battle. After the battle, the plinth will remain vacant.

I once had a dream of a funereal spartakiade on Wenceslas Square. I was watching it from above, having a bird's eye view, as often in my dreams before my view comes closer, zooming in like a camera, and I suddenly find myself at ground level. It happened to be the women's exercise sequence. They were in black costumes, even their heads were wound round with black scarves, recalling the veil of St Ludmilla, her, whose widowhood was lonesome and whom... (seen from the Museum, her statue is on Wenceslas' right). They were exercising with black muslin scarves which declined to flutter in the still air, just hanging limply in the hands of the women, whose movements were unbelievably slow, as in a slow-motion film. They dropped slowly to their knees and slowly rose again. I was watching from Dům potravin, the specialist food-store that stood at the spot now intersected by the inner ring road. The first line of gymnasts stood a few yards from me, I looked into the women's faces, but their faces expressed nothing, not even grief.

I had that dream in early August 1968. When later, on 21 August, tanks entered the City and blood flowed down from Radio House to Wenceslas Square, I wasn't standing by Dům potravin as in the dream. This time I woke to my first day in Paris and day after day I watched the action unfold on television, like a drama the words of which I barely understood. In that serial the City lay in ruins, I was afraid that the house opposite Olšany Cemetery was also in ruins, and also the house on George of Poděbrady Square. And when I later heard my parents' voice on the telephone (Stay there, don't come back!), it was the voice of people buried under rubble.

I did go back. The gun-barrels of tanks were poking out in squares and at the ends of streets like the long necks of antediluvian beasts. The City was not in ruins, as in the television drama, both the houses in my life were standing, my parents were alive, and a long and tortuous dying lay ahead of them. St Wenceslas had not abandoned his plinth, perhaps the blood running from Radio House hadn't reached the first step of the monument. The blood of Marie Charousková, Jan Bavorovský, Milan Kadlec and others (perhaps it was their names the old man at the PRAHA 1968 exhibition in the Museum was trying to decipher) made only little puddles. Someone had soaked a flag in one of them and put it in the bronze saint's hand (hadn't I seen that flag at the exhibition?). At the time, the statue had not yet been chained off, it could still serve as an altar on which relics could be assembled and at which a national requiem could be held.

And some months later, at the very spot where I had dreamed I stood during that funereal spartakiade, Jan Palach burst into flame.

Even then the statue failed to stir, perhaps because it had its back to the scene, that auto-da-fé. A few days after, I was on the tram, travelling through Wenceslas Square, and suddenly a wondrous scene emerged before me out of the dark. The fountain beneath the Museum, switched off in winter, was lit up by a multitude of candles. A confusion of bodies formed a *tableau vivant*. Atop the human pyramid shone a white mask on a black background.

Here I am, writing about that tableau and, by coincidence, I dreamed about Wenceslas Square again last night. Again I was standing at that spot by Dům potravin. No, no gymnastic display this time, no act of memorial. It was deserted, although it was broad daylight, possibly first thing in the morning. And yet there was something very odd. Between the Museum and Mezibranská Street, roughly where the Arena had stood in the nineteenth century, lay the skeleton of a whale. Until then, that skeleton had been exhibited in one of the halls of the National Museum, but some current had cast it up on the bank of the Square during the night. Then I noticed that a boy was running in circles round the white skeleton of the giant mammal. It was the boy from the Municipal Museum. I looked about me to see if the old man wasn't also somewhere nearby, but could see him nowhere.

ON CHARLES' BRIDGE

The time will come, the Blind Boy prophesied, when not a Czech will be seen on Prague Bridge. Czechs will be as rare as golden stags. Not a word of Czech will be heard. The Blind Boy's prophecy is coming true, you cannot now hear a word of Czech on the bridge, you cannot see a single Czech (no, there is one left, he's selling Soviet officers' caps, foreigners place them on their heads, laughing, and parade up and down the bridge in them). But then I take a closer look and see that among those laughing foreigners in officers' caps some people are crawling along on their knees. They're grovelling the whole length of the bridge, but most of those on their knees are huddled around the statue of a saint above whose head is a halo with five stars. And some people are leaning far out over the parapet to see the spot where the King had the Saint cast into the river for not revealing the secrets of the confessional. At least that is how the people interpret the dispute between Wenceslas IV and John Nepomucene.

I lean over the parapet and see the saint's body floating on the surface of the Vltava. And now I can also hear music, riverboats appear, decorated and aglow with many torches, and from the boats comes music. And as I continue along the bridge I observe how many stalls there are, selling miniature tongues of the Silent One. And they even have a little hummock with a flower, out of its bloom there grows – would you believe it! – a little tongue in wax.

I look about me to see if I can spot, among the pilgrims, Tereza Krebs, to whom the Saint appeared when she was sorely indisposed, he was in his canonicals with a fur around his shoulders, gazing vaguely upwards with impassioned eyes. And now I do see Tereza Krebs, she has thrust her way through to the Saint, kneels at his feet and stares up at him with the same longing as, a little way on, St Luitgard looks up at the Saviour on the Cross; perhaps Tereza Krebs saw herself in the Saint.

"I was born on a Wednesday..." And as the people sing "... martyred on a Wednesday...", two men steal along the Bridge "... condemned on a Wednesday...". They are dragging something heavy, in several pieces, they throw them one by one into the water "... also drowned...". One piece lands near the lifeless body of the Saint, which is still bobbing on the surface as it is ruffled by the boats; something glints. The body is almost sliced through by the blade of the Pankrác axe, which the executioner's henchmen secretly hurled into the river in late April 1945, perhaps to prevent the axe revealing the executioners' names, perhaps to stop it speaking out like the golden spinning-wheel in Erben's ballad. ... *Your own stepsister you did slay, and tore her limbs and eyes away – whirr – an evil thread!*

I slowly thread my way along the Bridge among the tourists

33

and pious pilgrims who have assembled here from different times. I also slip quickly past Jaroslav Hašek, he's just climbed onto the parapet, pretending he's going to jump into the river (later, in the asylum, he will claim to be Ferdinand the Good-Hearted). I'm nearing the end of the Bridge, approaching the Old Town (Staroměstská) Bridge Tower. I freeze, what's that I see, surely it's… I look up. They're all hanging there, all twelve of them, one head, the head of Prokop Dvořecký of Olbramovice, is leaning out, threatening to drop off. For several centuries people have been looking for these heads, taken down from the tower only ten years after the executions in the Old Town Square and hidden in a secret place inside the Týn Church, yet here they are, still hanging up there.

THE WAY INTO THE UNDERWORLD

Once during my childhood we were taken with the after-school club to the catacombs underneath the City. The memory of it is very vague, but I'm sure it wasn't a dream. I remember the way into the catacombs was on some slope. Our feet slithered on stones covered in slime and mud. They didn't allow us to go in too deep, but I remember being told that the passage went all the way under the City. I don't know where that way in was, when I was a child all places that lay beyond the immediate vicinity of the house opposite the cemetery or the school in Chapayev (now again Jiří z Lobkovic) Square seemed terribly far away, *abroad*. The known world ended at Hagibor in one direction and Hotel Flora in the other. On the hotel's windowless back wall there used to be a huge painting of a brown shoe. I recently noticed that the outlines of the monster shoe are beginning to show through the several layers of paint meant to obliterate it.

I have been looking for that entrance to the catacombs all my life. I think it likely that it was somewhere in the side of that hill named after the gallows, even then overgrown with thriving elder bushes. In all probability it collapsed long ago. Maybe it's not far from the statue of the Minotaur of Žižkov, a weird creature, seemingly half lion, half boar, with a mangled horn on its head. I didn't know about it at the time, I expect the statue was unveiled later, perhaps it was dug up when they were building fall-out shelters inside the hill. Perhaps the labyrinth disgorged the statue one day, like when the National Museum once disgorged the skeleton of a whale overnight.

I have recently read several books that write about what lies beneath Prague, the one by Karel Ladislav Kukla even has a diagram. It transpires that there were three ways out of this underworld: one in Košíře, another on Gallows Hill (the Apache Gate) and the third under Old Town Square, where the main junction of the sewers was constructed. The entrance under the Square was *official* and was even embellished with a notice: ENTRANCE FOR FOREIGNERS, because the aldermen liked to introduce foreign visitors that way in order to admire the wonders of the Prague sewer system. It occurred to me that there was probably another entrance, possibly deliberately omitted from the diagram, under the Castle, perhaps entered via the tomb of the Bohemian kings in St Vitus' Cathedral.

It's a long time since I've been up Gallows Hill. In recent times, its once conspicuous mound with the semi-circle of trees that surrounded the one-time execution site, has practically disappeared under a confusion of new tower blocks among which Gipsy children play. I look for the Minotaur; it has disappeared. Was it really here, or had I originally seen it only in a magazine photograph?

An old lady in the ticket-office situated inside the Cathedral sells me a ticket. I descend the narrow stairs into the royal tomb. I'm not alone. Glued to the grille that separates the public from the sarcophagi of the kings (including Charles IV, Wenceslas IV and Rudolf II) there's a boy, I recognise him, it's the boy from the Municipal Museum. Near him an old man is trying to decipher the seating, or rather lying, plan of the coffins attached to the grille. I catch the smell of elder. Here, underground? I turn – behind me there is a rock, actually the torso of some statue, an animal statue, half-lion and half-boar with a mangled horn. So that's how it is...

I'm passing the St Wenceslas Chapel. If I could go inside, I would find my face cast by magic in one of the agates, but the entrance is cordoned off by a rope across which you can't see very far in. I turn. The boy and the old man still haven't come out, or they have disappeared above ground in the crowd of foreigners laying siege to the Cathedral. Somewhere here there's supposed to be a veraikon – a picture of the face of Christ as imprinted on Veronica's veil. I seek it in vain. Perhaps it is hanging in one of the many closed chapels, maybe it's in the part behind the altar, over there somewhere, where the overblown tomb of the Silent One glows. They opened the coffin once. In the oral cavity of the saint's skull they found a lump of soil and the tongue preserved... HIC EST LINGUA ILLA BENEDICTA DIVI JOHANNI NEPOMUCENI MARTYRIS... INCORRUPTA REPERTA FUIT... But what if the picture now hangs somewhere else altogether, at the other end of the City? If I stare hard at the bark of a tree, one of those that encircle the execution site on the hill, perhaps I might find the semi-distinct features of the Saviour's face in it.

VERAIKON

Legend has it that Christ, as he climbed up to Golgotha, wiped his face on a cloth handed to him by Veronica – and, lo and behold, his features can still be discerned, it is claimed, on the Turin Shroud. Art has been fascinated by these phenomena – let's not mince words, these miracles – especially since the Middle Ages, when painters delighted in portraying Christ's face in the form that came to be known as a veraikon. One veraikon hangs in St Vitus', but when I looked in recently I sought it in vain. A hieratic full-face portrait of the Saviour with its rigid features seems intended to bewitch or warn those who approach, like the heads of the Medusa over the homes of the ancient Greeks. With its sometimes almost naiviste schematicism a veraikon looks a bit like a target from an old-fashioned shooting gallery. One such travelling shooting gallery is still going the rounds in Bohemia and has spent several winters at the foot of the Church of the Sacred Heart. If you aim at and hit the Saviour's eye, a concealed mechanism is set in motion... What blasphemy! In the summer, a bus with videogames parked up close to the church wall. The strange sound that issues from its innards – the bubbling and whirring sound of rotating spheres (passers-by can sometimes catch a shout from one of the impassioned players) – bounces off the church wall. What's strange is that the echo is absolutely the same – the bubbling and whirring of the spheres – only the shouts of the teenagers don't come through. The other day, the sound merged with sounds from the church organ.

A city of doppelgangers and weird encounters, strange images. There in the heart of the City, which has become a market-place of Babel above which a skeleton rings its bell at regular intervals and two little panels open to reveal the apostles and the Saviour gesturing a blessing, and, nearby, Death beckons to a miser with his moneybag who tosses his head in token of his unwillingness to follow, at this spot, where the Old Town puppet-show and dance of death keep coming round and round (it always ends with a cock-crow, not unlike the sound that sometimes emerges from the videogames bus), on the second floor of the Town Hall, which survived the war as a torso, one summer afternoon a face suddenly appears before the astonished crowd. This time the imprint is on paper and, unlike a veraikon, is three-dimensional, the image has been transformed into a relief – as if under pressure from *another* dimension, which is beginning to seep into the City through this very spot and at this very moment. Seep? Break out! A death mask? No – a living or perhaps dying mask with features of suffering and anguish, yet not a mask now, a very being, thrusting through the paper into existence. And other beings are literally unfurling – coming into being – from the roll of paper unrolled right down to the spectator's feet. How fragile, transitory these beings are! The principle of the veraikon and the Turin Shroud seems to have taken over almost everything. All around, nothing but imprints transferred from a tormented soul (one reminded me of... no, never mind), shapes kneaded and harried by the will of *another* world, which at once eagerly invades our secular world through every tear and pinhole and begins to...

I am coming back out into the sunlight and find myself in the thick of a medley of voices and languages. Opposite the entrance to the Staré Město Town-Hall obtrudes a work of art – a gold-painted Trabant on four giant paws. A little further on, in Charles (Karlova) Street, next to the theatrical supplies shop, I am suddenly seized by an odd feeling – through my body *another* body is forcing its way to the surface, through my face a face from Adriena Šimotová's exhibition is starting to luminesce.

BATTLE

In this City, things have recently begun leaving the places where they belong (or is it happening only in this writing?), much as times have begun to permeate one another (or am I merely becoming more susceptible to a phenomenon that has always been here?). And just as things migrate, so do figures and pictures. I would not be much surprised if I came out of the Museum underground station one day and found Marold's panorama of the Battle of Lipany in front of me, instead of in its customary place in Stromovka Park. It has come to rest there among all the fairground attractions, between the swan merry-go-round and the haunted castle, where a giant skeleton in a black cape leans far out of a window set in a tower like the Saviour on the astronomical clock. The path to the Panorama takes you past the ladies lavatories. The clamour of the fair is catapulted at the circular, fanciful picture capturing the final stage of the battle the Hussites lost (the traitor, Čapek ze Sán, is fleeing with his horsemen). The firmament above Lipany is collapsing, as has happened several times since the picture was installed, and when it rains puddles form on the battlefield.

I am standing on the ramp in front of the Museum overlooking the fountain that has long ceased to play and I am looking at that illusive picture. In the distance, at the spot where they opened the Forum coffee-house after the 1989 revolution and where street theatre is occasionally performed on the tiniest of stages (in the past, during May Day parades, a rostrum would stand there decked in red fabric), I can see the fleeing horsemen of the treacherous Čapek ze Sán. A number of banners can be made out – on one a chalice, on another a veraikon, on the third – from this distance I can't make the symbol out, though I'm looking through opera-glasses. Oh, but it's… now I see it – the face of the king-prisoner or prisoner-king from Calderón's play that has been put on for some time now in this City. In the picture there's even an overturned cart – a tank rolled onto its side. A little further on, as in the picture in Stromovka Park, there is a dilapidated wayside cross and, nearby, where Franz Kafka's one-time employer, the Assicurazioni Generali insurance company, used to be, there is a gallows. There isn't one in Marold's picture in Stromovka Park (after all, in those days the victors would drive captured Hussites into a barn and set fire to it). And I can see another, and another… a forest of gallows has sprung up on the Square after the rain, which has got into the picture through holes in the firmament. Only then do I notice that where the statue of St Wenceslas with his retinue of patron saints used to stand there is a gaping void. Perhaps the statue of the saint murdered at the cathedral threshold has come to life, blood has reached the first step of the monument… I have a sense that if I were to look down now at the fountain I would see the white death-mask of the young man who stepped into the fiery furnace outside Dům potravin.

The clamour of the fair being held on Wenceslas Square is catapulted into the picture, actually several pictures at once. Not far from the overturned tank, which has become one of the fairground attractions, they're playing that old French farce, *Everything, Nothing and Everyman*. An actor in a dark cape with a white skeletal mask is reciting: "Each rips the flesh from the other's body." After each line he beats his drum: "That's how it's done. And their eyes from their sockets" (drumroll), "Now they're shouting more and more. What's going on? Nothing at all." A buxom woman in a gold bra lifts Mánes' astronomical clock above the audience's head – no, it's a Wheel of Fortune. A rag-doll clown is lashed to the wheel, his legs dangle in a funny way as Everything turns the wheel. By turns the clown is at the top, where Everything sets a tiny crown on his head, and at the bottom, where the crown falls off. I thrust my way closer to the stage. "Everyone and Everything now stride towards Nothing," the woman recites and turns the wheel to make the clown's head hang down again. "That ending signifies doubtless that Dame Fortune is our mistress," another actor is reciting now, I hadn't noticed him before, "and she dulls our senses." He is very like the clown on the wheel, they have the same hooked nose. Finally, I am right next to the stage, directly beneath the wheel of Fortune. And then I see that there are tarot cards on it, and can recognise them now. Here's the king with a crown on his head, actually an emperor, and beneath him is the pagato, the first card in the set, the magician and the creator, and there's death, the only one unnamed. "In the end, Everything comes to Nothing. Our life proceeds in just this way. Take it, please, ye cannot gainsay." The last words of the play are spoken by the skeleton or Nothing, with a sweep of the hand it rips off its white mask, beneath it... At that moment the mask reminds me of another mask, the one at the Museum. Or is it one and the same?

I move on, more drumming behind me, someone, perhaps Everything, is playing the flute. A new performance will be starting soon. "I'm here, or there, by night and day... I am but spun by the wind at play." The Wheel of Fortune is now turning for a new audience, behind me the clown dangles his rag legs. Outside the former House of Silk they're erecting a stand. Or could it be a

fairground Haunted Castle, out of which Nothing will lean? Is it
a memory? A prophecy?

MADWOMAN

Years ago I used to meet her on National Avenue. She was one of
Prague's characters. She might have been the embodiment of all
those seduced and abandoned women with which nineteenth-cen-
tury Czech literature so abounds, the most famous being Božena
Němcová's deranged Viktorka. Last century Bridge (Mostecká)
Street in Malá Strana was the haunt of Crazy Terezka. She had
been seduced and then abandoned by a Prussian officer, set off
into the wide, wide world to look for him, came back, they say,
after a year and then, out of her mind, roamed the streets of Malá
Strana until her death. They called her *Queen of Prussia*. I recently
read in a magazine about the Countess. Her great-grandmother,
she insists, had been a Spanish infanta. The Countess was carried off by an SS-man to Ravensbrück, then when he'd had his
fill of her he passed her on to others. Today she is over eighty.
She's even had a part in a film. You can tell her by her blond wig,
extraordinary clothes and tall hat. Made up like a puppet, she
wanders Staré Město. Maybe there's something in the air of this
City that at given intervals, every fifteen or twenty years, engen-
ders these deranged characters, seduced and abandoned, much
as, according to Jewish legend, the Golem appears in the ghetto
every thirty years. I expect that even that crazed old lady I used
to meet in National Avenue in the early 1970s was a product of
the City's atmosphere. Ahead of her she would push a battered,
ramshackle pram, in which a doll with its eyes closed lay in a
confusion of dirty rags.

I recently met that madwoman again, perhaps time goes into a
warp during these months. Her, or some other, whose story had
just entered its final stage. The point is, all these creatures are as
alike as peas in a pod. I met her outside the Albatros publishing

house. This time, too, she was pushing a dilapidated pram that hobbled on one wheel. In it was the same confusion of rags, beneath which was the hump of a doll, but its face wasn't visible. The old lady looked neither right nor left, so she kept bumping her pram into people, who them hurled abuse at her. "You mad old hag!" And suddenly an apple came flying through the air, probably thrown by the little girl standing outside that shop with the sign in Spanish, CASA PASCUAL, and landed straight in the pram. The old lady let out a groan and pounced on the uncovered doll. Then I saw its face. It had a dusky-olive, dark colour, its southern eyes seeming to turn away from the alien, hostile people. It struck me as familiar, where had I seen that face before? As the old lady's trembling hands fiddled with the rags and tried to wrap the doll in them (amazingly, she didn't even notice the apple, which had a bite out of it, she left it lying next to one waxy-yellow little hand), a bit of blue fabric glinted in the pram, perhaps gold-brocade. After wrapping the doll, head and all, she proceeded on her way, drove her pram under the arcade, two or three lonely candles were still burning there. Then she must have turned into the Metro Palace passage, because I lost sight of her.

I couldn't shake off the image of that doll. Not until the night, when I couldn't get to sleep, did it dawn. The next day I set off at once. Fortunately the church was open, the congregation was gathering for evening service. There it was, standing in its silver case with its glass doors. It has a crown on its head, it is holding an orb (which in Czech is a 'royal apple') in its left hand, giving a blessing with its right, averting its gaze from the strangers. Its little face is dusky-olive, strikingly southern, after all it comes from Spain. That day it was dressed (on certain days they re-dress it) in a green gown, which, as the inscription says, was embroidered by none other than Empress Maria Theresa. The statuette is said to have lain, during the Thirty Years' War, among the junk behind the altar with its arms knocked off until it was found by a monk, Cyril, and then it started performing miracles. Now it stands radiant in all its beauty in the Church of Our Lady of Victories in Malá Strana, but during the day, when the church is closed, a crazy old lady drives the Bambino di Praga, that Infant Jesus of Prague, around the City in her pram.

EXAMINATION

I entered the Jewish quarter one more time, that was almost twenty years back. The recollection of that experience of long ago has only surfaced now. At the time, Nina V. and I were waiting in the corridor on the topmost, fifth, floor of the Arts Faculty, the last candidates for the puppet theatre exam. It was getting quite late, evening, night may have already fallen. By then, the faculty building was almost deserted. We had begun to feel that Dr B. had forgotten about us, we weren't even sure whether there was anyone inside. Suddenly, the door flew open and Dr B. appeared in the doorway of the Theatre Cabinet. He was asking us to help him, one girl had collapsed during her exam. His arms flailed helplessly.

She was lying in the middle of the room, which had always captured my attention with its miniature models of stage sets (if memory serves, one of them was of the last act of *Libuše*, where the princess prophesies glory to the Czechs), her dark hair was spread out around her head like a veil. She had tried to commit suicide, at least that was what she had threatened Dr B. After I wiped her brow with a damp handkerchief she stirred. She said she had first meant to jump out of the window, but when he prevented her she had swallowed some pills. I went across to the window. Only then did I realise that that way did not lie the river and Red Army Square (the bed of red flowers in the middle of it forms a five-pointed star) and that therefore you cannot see the familiar panorama of Prague from it. The window of the Theatre History Cabinet opens onto Broad Street and from it you get a glimpse of the Old Jewish Cemetery with its floundering gravestones; the oldest, fifteenth-century, belongs to Rabbi Avigdor Karó, the elegist of the pogrom in the ghetto. So this was the direction – I

43

thought – in which the girl (we didn't know her and we hadn't even noticed her out in the corridor) meant to jump, because she had failed her exam in puppet theatre.

We went with her in the ambulance to the František Hospital intensive care department, where suicides are taken. She came round in the ambulance and looked at us slightly surprised with her Semitic eyes. The dose of barbiturates couldn't have been very large, she soon came out of the department into the corridor, only her face was a slightly paler shade than it had been. As we walked her down the corridor towards the exit, I had no inkling that I would soon be walking down the same corridor, the floor of which is popularly believed to be made of planks from the Old Town gallows, to see my dying mother.

She didn't want us to call a taxi, she was feeling better now and could easily get home, not far away, on foot. And it really wasn't far, she lived in Maisel Street, near the Old-New Synagogue. My impression of that visit is now very hazy. Even at that advanced hour, three little girls, her younger sisters – Fegal, Hyndl and Plumel – were still running around the flat, which was cluttered up with a lot of bulky furniture. And she was Hana, Hana Kalman, her sisters called her Hanina. All over the flat, which, because it was so crammed full of furniture separated by narrow, sharp-angled aisles, was oppressive, there were all sorts of hangings, you might say arrases, apparently concealing other little nooks and crannies. I don't know why it came to me then that on the other side of the wall, or one of those embroidered curtains with flowers, vases and mysterious symbols, was my grandfather Jerie's surgery, after all, in the early 1950s his surgery *was* here, in Maisel Street, but at the time I was very small and I couldn't now remember the house. I imagined that if I drew aside one of those curtains, perhaps the blue one with silver embroidery and a purple hem, grandfather's surgery would be revealed, his monstrous gynaecological chair, which had so frightened me as a child, would glint out of the darkness.

Hanina was apparently still befuddled from the pills she had

44

taken and kept rambling. Was she not saying something about being a rabbi's daughter and that she had been carried off by the water king she had fallen in love with (I don't know whether she meant Dr B.)? She was expecting his baby. She stroked her belly and only then did we notice that she was pregnant, her wide skirt of a dark heavy material (when we complimented her on it she said she had made it out of an old Sabbath table-cloth) concealed her little bulge. And when her time came, she would be helped by old Mrs Šifrová in Narrow Lane, she wouldn't go to the maternity hospital, suppose they swapped her baby for another? I very nearly suggested that she go and see my grandfather, that his surgery was somewhere nearby, possibly next door, he could deliver the child (the water king's, or Dr. B.'s?). It was a ridiculous idea, of course, if only because by then my grandfather had been dead for several years. Perhaps I too was befuddled by that unusual course of events and my thinking likewise a little bit mad. And I might also have been affected by Hanina's special charm, from time to time, with some ancient ritual gesture, she would smooth the skirt made of a Sabbath table-cloth where it covered her belly and fix us with her dark, Semitic eyes. She told us things and all the while her younger sisters Fegal, Hyndl and Plumel (rather surprisingly I have remembered those names, they were so unusual) kept hopping all around us like the tame squirrels in Olšany Cemetery.

Then we forgot all about Hanina Kalman, who probably dropped out of her theatre studies course, if she ever even took it. The Jewish quarter, into which we intruded on that occasion, again passed from our awareness or became simply closed off to us who are *goyim*. Years later, I discovered the story of Hanina, the daughter of Rabbi Kalman, abducted by the water king, in Herrmann and Teige's book on the Prague ghetto. The name of old Mrs Šifrová was also there. Had Hanina's ravings been calculated, or was it that that old Jewish legend had come remarkably to life in her semi-conscious state? Or was it that as she thought up that fairy-tale, she had no idea that she was recounting one of

the Jewish legends? Or was it I who brought the whole story to
life having touched the shem on her brow with my handkerchief?

OLD TOWN SQUARE

That day, early in the morning, there are said to have been two
rainbows arching over Prague, *for the sky was clear, there having
been no rain for two days before or afterwards…* (The Story of
the Great Tribulations). The city gates remained closed. On the
stroke of five some cannon shots rang out through Prague. At
that moment, the black-hooded beadle mounted the gallows and
placed a black cross on the staging…

Our class was standing not far from the John Huss monument,
not at the point where, to the right of the preacher, towering above
the dying fire, the closed ranks of Hussites with their shields
and flails have formed a wall, but to his left, facing the execution
site where the people, humiliated by their enslavement after the
Battle of the White Mountain, cringe at Huss's feet. From where
we stood we couldn't see over the mass of heads to the platform
draped in red cloth, nor could we see the face of whoever happened to be speaking.

The condemned men were mounting the platform in order of
family standing, rank and age, first the lords, then the knights and
finally the burghers. Their last words were lost in the clangour of
drums and trumpets.

Suddenly there was a dog beside us, a big dog and gaunt. He
rubbed against my coat, then ambled off. The crowd parted to
make way for him, so the dog probably made it all the way to the
platform. There was a doleful howl, above which the president's
speech droned unwavering on from the loudspeakers. Then I saw
the dog being led off by two grey-uniformed men of the People's
Militia with machine-guns, they were dragging the animal by
the leather belt that one of them had taken off. Without a word,
people made way for this most peculiar procession.

"The February victory of the working people has created the conditions for the construction of a socialist..." At that point, in the scenario of the 1621 executions on Old Town Square, the public executioner had taken his tongs to pull out and grip the tongue of Jan Jesenius, Rector of Prague University. And at that very moment in 1962 a pillar of fire leapt up from the Huss monument. The crowd shrank away from the statue. Then he cut Jesenius' tongue out and sank his axe into his neck. "The people have taken power into their own hands." Some people passed by us carrying a charred body wrapped in a coat and others led away those who were groaning from their burns, their faces blackened. "On that day, on this very spot, Comrade Klement Gottwald..."

Dr Jesenius' body was carted off the same day to a point outside Upper Gate, where the executioner quartered it. *Then he bore up the twelve heads, Šlik's with one hand to his mouth, Budovec's, Kaplíř's, Dvořecký's – from Bílá, Otto's, Michalovec's with his hand placed upon his head, Kochán's, Štefka's, Kober's, Jesenius' with a piece of his tongue, Haunšild's, also with his hand on his head, onto the bridge tower opposite the Jesuit College.* As I was dragged along by the crowd leaving the square after the speech, almost running along Iron (Železná) Lane, I saw the dog again. He was lying close by a wall, in front of a shop-window display of ivory statuettes, and a trickle of blood was coming out of his mouth.

That evening we watched television, where they repeated the President's entire speech. We watched his face closely. It remained immobile even at the moment when he was talking about the February victory, when the executioner was pulling Dr Jesenius' tongue out and a pillar of fire shot up from Huss's pyre. Or was there just a hint of a waver before it froze again into the expression of a mask of indifference? A few days later, at the Pražačka grammar school that I attended, two men appeared with huge photographs of a sea of heads. On the transparencies placed over the photographs we were to identify our heads. The papers carried not a word of the event. It was said that fortunately only the primer of the bomb had gone off – otherwise the whole of

Old Town Square, Town Hall and execution site and all, would have been razed to the ground. The scorching heat of the flame from the Huss monument had only seared my face slightly.

On 2nd June 1990 a bomb went off at the same spot. Fragments injured several children playing nearby and one entered the eye of a German lady tourist, who had been drinking coffee. Whenever I walk along Iron Lane, I see him there lying beneath the statuettes of Indian deities. Lying on his flank close to the wall, a trickle of blood coming out of his mouth.

IN GOLDEN LANE

I am struggling through the crowds of tourists in Golden Lane (Zlatá ulička). This little street looks like a model for a puppet theatre. I am struck by the notion that one day it will be a street of clockwork figures. Tourists will enter the tiny houses and look into the tiny rooms. An alchemist shakes a retort containing a mysterious liquid, in the corner an athanor is smoking away, above the door – so low that visitors must mind their heads – stands the magic inscription: VISITA INTERIORA TERRAE RECTIFICANDO INVENIES OCCULTUM LAPIDEM. The more attentive observer will notice that, lying entwined inside the retort, there is a tiny king and queen, from whose union will be born... In another house they will be minting old Bohemian groschen bearing a likeness of Charles IV, the coins, red-hot from the furnace, will hiss as Jiří Hovorka (his name will be hung over the door) – clockwork puppet or flesh and blood? – tosses them into a tub of water. And in No. 22, to which tourists will particularly throng, Franz Kafka will be sitting at a table (they'll easily recognise him by his projecting ears), lying in front of him will be a sheet of paper with a scene from, say, St Vitus' Cathedral. He will dip his pen in the ink, bend his head and write, time and again he will write the selfsame scene from his novel, knowing no other (the sheet will be sold for $5). And the other houses will also have occupants, of whom no one will be sure whether they are dummies or people. And shuffling down the street, bumping into the tourists, will come the insane Professor Uhle, who moved from Vienna to Golden Lane in the 1820s and performed his alchemical experiments here. On Whit Sunday 1831 there was an explosion during one of his experiments and the professor died in the fire. And the tourists won't know whether he too is an actor or a dummy as they throw coins into his hat and touch his scruffy, buttonless coat. And right at the end of the lane, No. 14 will once more be home to a fortune-teller and clairvoyant, the widow who calls herself Madame de Thèbes.

I enter No. 14. Madame de Thèbes is sitting at a table laid for dinner – for her and her son, missing in the First World War (his bed in the little upper room is made up as every evening), although by now the Second World War has broken out – and still today, at the end of the millennium, when the clairvoyant has changed into a puppet. At the front door ladies try on her hat with its ostrich feathers. Above Madame de Thèbes's head hangs a hexagram.

WILL

HATRED

FALSEHOOD

LOVE

TRUTH

CAPRICE

Someone speaks, it is Madame de Thèbes: This is that cloth of six threads that flies as the flag of the Velvet Revolution, which will culminate in free elections in 1990. That year is the last and most powerful in the eleven-year period of the Sun's activity. $1 + 9 + 9 + 0 = 19$. The number 19 is borne by the tarot trump card called Sun, Horus, Child. Thus does Madame de Thèbes read the signs. Can she see the future and yet not know that her son will not be coming back? That's the point, she can... (Copies of the hexagram, as reproduced by Soluna, may be purchased in the adjacent house for $10.)

By night the puppets remain alone in their little houses, sitting in the dark, in their appointed places. Only Jiří Hovorka – he's not a clockwork puppet after all – takes himself off home to Jižní Město. Franz Kafka will become rigid over his scene in the cathedral, unless he's seized with a hacking cough during the night. Madame de Thèbes sits at her table laid for dinner, her son didn't arrive today either. She won't be able to sleep, anxious in case the Germans come for her again in the night, "... foretelling the end of the war, Frau Průšová, das ist verboten" (for the time being prophesying revolution *is* permitted), again they will take her off to Bredovská Street, hang her up by the feet and beat her. A puppet? Visitors to No. 14 will not learn what became of Madame de Thèbes, it would be a pity if Golden Lane were to become Torment Lane.

IN ST NICHOLAS CHURCH

It was late October and I was on my way back to the Castle. I wanted to take a look at St Wenceslas' chasuble in the Chapel of the Holy Cross. Originally I had been taken by the notion that the fabric design on the jacket of this book came from Charles IV's shroud. However, the cloth has lost its colour and where once there were stylised bunches of grapes, that symbol of Christ's salvation, but also of initiation into the mysteries of life after death, there are now holes. I had also thought of the shred of the vestment (or antependium) of St Wenceslas, which I had seen in the Municipal Museum, but that, as I was told by the experts, had been damaged through inept restoration. For technical reasons, the Chapel of the Holy Cross was closed, so I did not see

St Wenceslas' chasuble.

I was descending the Castle Steps. In my childhood, but in later life too, I didn't know where the steps would take me, there are two sets (or even three?), one leads down to Klárov and the Wallenstein (Valdštejn) riding-school, the other to St Nicholas' and Malá Strana Square (and the third?). And this time, perhaps because I was immersed in thought, I didn't know either. Suddenly, on the steps ahead of me, I spotted the Countess, it was definitely her, I recognised her from her striking tall hat and short skirt with its jazzy pattern. In Neruda Street, where the steps brought me out, I lost sight of the Countess among the crowds of foreigners heading for the Castle; I kept having to make way for them, stepping off the narrow pavement into the roadway.

Since I was in the area, it occurred to me I could pop into St Nicholas' to have a look at Balek's picture of the dying St Francis Xavier, which once so fascinated the hero of Arbes' *romanetto*. It was afternoon and, as in the *romanetto*, the rays of the sun were coming into the church from the south-west and the west-facing picture could be seen to its best advantage. On a deserted sea-shore a man in black monastic attire is dying. Half-lying, he is reclining on a rough reed mat, his back resting against a rock. In one hand he is holding a crucifix, the other hangs limply from his bed. His deep-set eyes are turned to Heaven and are drowning in the light of the sun, which is either about to rise or has just set.

I went and sat in a confessional from where I had a better view of the picture. The people who had congregated for the afternoon service were leaving the church, the priest had withdrawn to the vestry and the sacristan, jangling a bunch of keys, was heading at a leisurely pace away from the high altar. He passed me at close quarters without noticing me in the darkness of the confessional. But I could see him. It was my father and the whole scene in the church was a scene in the film in which he played the sacristan. Now, as in the book and the film, he should step up to the altar where the picture of St Francis Xavier is, a pale young man (he was played in the film by Viktor Preiss) in an elegant black suit, drop down on a hassock, lower his head into his hands. But no one came, only the sacristan returning from the entrance, he must have locked up, passing by me again, he did glance into the confessional, but either he didn't see me, or it struck him as entirely natural that I should be sitting there, maybe this was following a different script that I didn't know, or it was all going on in a dream that I had lapsed into in the confessional.

Suddenly, without being aware at precisely what moment it happened, I realised that for some time I hadn't been looking at the picture of the saint, which was in any case now sinking in darkness, but at a huge spherical contraption concealing the high altar. I got up and went slowly towards the object in the middle of the church. Only when I was but two steps away from it did I understand. It was a balloon – the balloon of Count Blanchard, who would rise (had risen?) in it high over Prague. Time had gone into another warp. Amazingly, the period was right, the balloon had been exhibited at the end of October 1790. Except that it was in a different church – St Nicholas', but the one in Staré Město. I touched the balloon cautiously with one finger (as once in a dream I had touched my dead mother who tried to convince me she was alive). That touch was enough for the balloon to begin to shrink before my very eyes (my mother's hand had been ice-cold). And as the balloon shrank, the light it had blocked fell once more on the picture. The eyes of the dying man now stared into the middle of the church, to the point where that magical scene had taken place, at the balloon, which was slowly losing its divine, spherical shape.

ABOVE THE CITY

It is said that Prague, the city in the basin cut in two by the Vltava, is, like Rome, spread over seven hills. In my dreams I mostly float over the City under the power of my arms and legs. This time, though, I was flying in a balloon.

I am trying to make out the various hills beneath me. – Look, Vyšehrad – *once the cradle and the tomb of kings, lies famous Vyšehrad*, wrote Karel Hynek Mácha. His body was transferred to Vyšehrad in 1939 – on the threshold of the years of darkness. Once upon a time the tomb of the Kings of Bohemia did lie here. On its flanks I can see the hundreds of dead from the battle that Emperor Sigismund fought with the Hussites and lost. The dead, who included twenty noble lords, were left on the battlefield as a warning and as food for birds of prey. At this very moment a two-tailed lion comes out of the rock where it guards the horsemen of Vyšehrad. It roars down into the valley, but no one replies, and so the beast goes back inside the rock to join the sleeping knights. It will only re-appear after a year has passed.

We fly on. Count Blanchard, he who flew across the English Channel and first sailed over Prague on 31 October 1790, shows me Petřín, amazed at the lookout tower on the top of the hill. "It's a small-scale version of the Eiffel Tower in Paris," says Count Šternberk, whom I had so far not registered in the balloon's basket, or *suspended gallery*. "From here on a clear day you can see the mountains far away on the frontiers." If memory serves, in a story by Věra Linhartová the astronomer Flammarion has taken up residence in Petřín tower (wasn't the person talking to him also flying in a balloon?). Long ago, at the spot where the tower now stands, you would have seen smoke rising from a pagan place of sacrifice, and where the mirror maze is today, and the diorama of the Defence of Prague against the Swedes in 1648, the Vršovci clan were executed. Places with a memory change into places for fairground attractions, history into illusive pictures.

We are flying over the hill called Sion, otherwise Strahov. In the courtyard, where as recently as yesterday stood a lion roaring, a bonfire seems to be burning. With the aid of the telescope kindly lent to me by Count Blanchard, I can see that what is burning are books. Every so often a monk bends down and tosses a volume into the fire. Do my eyes deceive me? Wasn't that Huss's *Postilla*, it flared up with a yellow flame? Now he is holding Comenius'

Labyrinth of the World and the Paradise of the Heart, then it too is cast into the flames, which at that instant turn purple. And now – can it be? – Karel Čapek's *Conversations with T. G. Masaryk*, they also end in the flames, which now turn green. Now the abbot supervising nods and the monks fork over the ashes – of Huss, Comenius, Čapek. Could this be a sign? After all, I know for a fact that the books of those Protestants, who are not to the liking of the Premonstratensians, are still in the Strahov Library; the monks have yet to return to the monastery, although their habits can be spotted more and more frequently in its dark corridors. "This is where the classrooms will be, and here (they were in the room where the photocopier stands today) the showers," said the Abbot.

On we fly. At the top of the steep slopes of a rocky hill stands an enclosed group of wooden dwellings – the seat of the princely family of the Přemyslides and their entourage. The image of the Castle changes swiftly, centuries pass in seconds. Rearing up towards us now is the Gothic cathedral, whose plans were conceived in the head of the master-builder of Avignon, Matthias of Arras, and at once I see the Cathedral engulfed in flames, and again… I can't follow the further metamorphoses of this illustrious place because the wind has suddenly caused the balloon to veer to the east. And now beneath us a gigantic Žižka on horseback has appeared, for we happen to be flying over Vítkov with its mausoleum of Communist presidents. In its day, the embalmed body of Klement Gottwald lay here like Snow White under a glass cover, but then they had to incinerate the body because it had begun to decompose, noxious matter was claimed to have leaked into the ground and contaminated the water in the Žižkov Baths.

The wind has begun to toss the balloon furiously from side to side. We career towards the new television tower, miss it by a whisker. A pair of birds of prey are circling its tip. The wind is now so strong that Count Blanchard decides to land at the nearest suitable place. The basket hits the ground hard.

I come round – after a moment? A year? I'm on some hill. I part the branches of an elder bush. I can't see the City, not even the famous panorama on the horizon. Just a few treeless knolls rise out of the water that has come up to the foot of the hill. Only now does it come back to me – we were flying in a balloon, we must have landed here, I seek the remains of the balloon in vain. Count Blanchard and Count Šternberk have also vanished. Perhaps the balloon has transported me in my sleep to some other land… I look about me. Behind me stands a semi-circle of trees, their crowns shaven conically. We have landed on Gallows Hill.

BENEATH THE CITY

I set off to investigate the hill. I have to force my way through the elder bushes, by now they have covered not just the slopes, but are approaching the crown of the hill from all sides, so that the ground-plan of the execution site is much less clear than previously. They are overgrowing the hill practically before my very eyes. The berries have already turned black and are giving off their heady smell, beginning to rot. It's how I imagine the smell of the plague. *Praga – plaga*, as the nickname went.

I find myself by the entrance that leads beneath ground. Once I had sought it in vain, now it was easy. Someone had cleared the obstruction, probably Counts Blanchard and Šternberk – they must have been here before me. Right at the entrance on a pile of rotten corpses lay an animal. The Minotaur? – A dog, large, gaunt. It gets up the moment I approach. But surely, it's… The immortal dog trots a little way ahead of me down the sloping passageway.

I cannot shake off a sense of repeating someone else's journey, I am ceasing to be myself, at this very moment, as my peregrination through the City is – I get the feeling – coming to a close, I am becoming two, like all else in this accursed space. Then above me I hear that inimitable sound, that strange squeaky noise that's supposed to be the crowing of a cock. So I'm beneath Old Town Square, there must be a way out somewhere here, on the outside there may still be that notice ENTRANCE FOR FOREIGNERS.

But the dog doesn't stop, it runs on and I trust to its instinct. Now and again I think I can hear the distant rumble of underground trains (does the City live on under water?). Now I know, I'm following in the footsteps of Libuše – Princess Libuše, or the Libuše Moníková of *Pavane for a Dead Infanta*? She followed a lion, I'm following a dog.

We've been going uphill for some time. I think we must be somewhere under Chotek Road, the passageway forms a loop here. Now I expect we're beneath the Belvedere (the song of the fountain doesn't reach this far down), and now we could be close to the royal tomb, whither the Minotaur of Žižkov has withdrawn. But the dog trots ever onwards. At last it stops. I lift the hatch, surprisingly it isn't at all heavy. We are – in the gents' lavatory. We come out. As I entered the underworld on Gallows Hill it had been daylight. Now it is night, the journey has taken much longer than it seemed. Either the water must have receded or it doesn't reach this far. I mount the steps. GOLDEN LANE – GOLDENGASSE. The tiny houses like houses for the puppets of the Dragon (Drak) Theatre… But why here? What can I be being told by a pilgrimage that ends in these parts? The dog begins quietly howling. It lies down beside No.22. Its body twitches once or twice, then the end comes. A trickle of blood comes out of his mouth.

IN THE VLTAVA

My migration was not yet at an end. After ordeal by fire, air and earth, there remained ordeal by water. I don't know how I ended up in the water. It was murky, but surprisingly warm. I was swimming just below the surface. My strokes made no sound. In front of me a stone wall appeared, a massive bridge pier. In this City there is only one bridge with piers like this, I thought. I surfaced. And indeed, to the right were the outlines of a bridge tower, perhaps on the Old Town side, there was also one to the left. But that way there should be two of them... If this were that bridge, then somewhere to the right should be that mysterious head set in the embankment wall, Beardy, actually only a copy, after all I had recently seen the original head in the Municipal Museum. But why need I look for the bearded head, I can tell it's this bridge from the statues, perhaps the group statue of St Luitgard, to whom Christ crucified appeared in a dream, or the statue of St John Nepomucene with five stars in his halo, who appeared in a dream to Tereza Krebs. And suddenly it hits me that there are no statues on the bridge. Could it be Judith's Bridge, the one that stood here before Charles' Bridge? Or won't the statues come to me in sleep? Am I dreaming?

I headed for the left bank, which was closer. There I should find a statue of the knight Bruncvík, a knight in armour resting on his sword, a lion at his feet, I remember that statue well. But the knight wasn't where he should be either. On the other hand, a little way off from the bank sat an old man in a boat, fishing perhaps. Hardly had I hauled myself into the boat, he pulled on the oars and the boat lurched into the current. He might have been hurrying to get as quickly as possible out of sight of the rubberneckers who were now leaning out over the parapet of the bridge.

"I'll take you for a little ride, Hanina, before you go back home." I wasn't even surprised that he didn't ask me how I had got into the river, perhaps this wasn't the first time he had waited for me. We turned into a narrow backwater and immediately passed under a bridge. We were at Kampa Island. The boat now moved on its own, almost floating over the surface. Then came the outlines of the mill wheel, to my surprise it was turning, I had last seen it turn some time in the early 1960s. Since then it had been standing there as a broken-down attraction and gradually falling into decay. We aimed for the wheel. I felt fear. "Don't be afraid, Hanina, it's like riding the Wheel of Fortune." I was seized with anxiety, but there wasn't time to jump out of the boat and I didn't have the strength anyway. Now the wheel had picked us up and carried us aloft and then we travelled back down on it and sailed on through beneath the surface. It was like the Big Wheel at the St Matthew's Fair in Stromovka Park. We took a few turns on the wheel, then I suddenly noticed that the old fisherman looked like my father, who died six years ago. Then we took a few more turns on the wheel, and I suddenly discovered I was alone in the boat, no, I wasn't in the boat, I was clutching the wheel and the wheel continued describing its circular motion with me on it. I was too afraid to jump off, and at the same time I longed to go back. To the house opposite Olšany Cemetery, which I had left to enter this City forty-four years ago? To the waking world? To my own existence? But I was a prisoner of the wheel in Devil's Stream (Čertovka), I was rotating in the life of that girl from the ghetto who once jumped into the Vltava for love of the water king. On the heavy material of the long skirt I was now wearing a strange, alien pattern was beginning to show.

AT KARLOV

Foreigners are alighting from their coaches and heading in droves to the Chalice pub, from where Jaroslav Hašek embarked on his legendary journey to the Great War. I am passing the asylum in St Katherine's Convent. Twenty years ago I would accompany my mother here every Sunday evening, she suffered from endogenous depression. Then from Monday to Friday she would look out of a window in the ward onto the hospital garden, onto which, from the other side, from Purkyně's house, Albert Einstein would look and work out his theory of relativity. In the end, a tumor grew on my mother's brain and they only discovered it when it was the size of an apple. To this day they are looking at each other – the famous physicist and my insane mother, both long dead.

A man in overalls is coming towards me with a hold-all over his shoulder. "Folo! Folo!" A tradesman? A madman? What does *folo* mean?

The street of madmen fills with the roar of the beer-exalted patrons of the Chalice. I think I spotted someone in fancy dress by the entrance. Could it be a carnival, now, in September? Perhaps the pub has revived an old custom for the benefit of foreign tourists, in celebration of Bacchus, perhaps they celebrate him every day. Bacchus, in a flowing red cape, a paper crown on his head, is sitting atop a huge barrel, he drinks beer all day and pontificates, by evening he just babbles. Hovering around Bacchus there is a Jew in a black coat down to his ankles. I wonder if the man shouting *folo* is part of that fancy-dress do at the Chalice.

I enter the church at Karlov, it rears up on its promontory like the last outpost of suicides, a place of salvation before the abyss, before the jump from the high bridge arching over the deep valley. The rail of the bridge is very low, it doesn't take much and a body can pitch itself into the abyss (like the body of the theatre specialist Vladimír M.) and shatter down below in many pieces. And see, there inside is Christ standing before Pilate. In a window of the house opposite, three figures are gesticulating excitedly, two men and a buxom woman. They remind me of the actors in that old French farce that is performed on Wenceslas Square outside the Forum. All they're missing is the Wheel of Fortune and the man at the back still hasn't donned a black cape, still hasn't pulled on a white mask so there can be no doubting that Nothing… No, it isn't them, they are just tinted statues of spectators, a *trompe l'œil*. Next to them on the balcony the scene of the Visitation is being played out. Here in this church, too, various dimensions of time exist simultaneously. And there is one other sacred scene here, down below.

I want to go down to the crypt, but the door is shut, protected by a grille. NATIVITY UNDER RECONSTRUCTION. Last time I was there, the candle flames were flickering in a subterranean draught. Nearby, underground trains passed, I could hear the rumble they made, growing louder as they entered the tunnel under the roadway on the bridge. With every passing moment the Child is born in the grotto to the rumbling of trains. And today?

By the church wall lies a rag-covered figure. A person? A statue under restoration? I suddenly hear shouting and drumming. The fancy-dress crowd. You can hear them even here. But they're the actors that the statues in the window of the house reminded me of just now. Could they be going to perform in the church? Perhaps they have already been performing at the Chalice, they're tottering about among the pews as if drunk. They're fighting over something, gesticulating excitedly. The younger man is pointing towards Pilate's house, the older one – Nothing – takes him by the arm, his cape is probably in the knapsack on his back, I expect he's got his mask in it as well. Where have they left the Wheel of Fortune? The actor who plays Everyone in the farce comes running out of the church, heads for the bridge. I hope he isn't going to jump … ! The other two run after him – the woman in the gold bra and Nothing, who pulls his cape on as he runs. Shortly, I see all three back again. All with their arms round the others' shoulders. They are laughing, so it was just play-acting.

PILGRIMAGE

I met her again on National Avenue, this time outside the Platýz. She might have popped up out of the passage, since suddenly there she was, a few paces ahead of me. She was staring into her pram, which is why she kept bumping into people in the crowd streaming along National Avenue that late afternoon. I was close behind her and this time she didn't disappear in the Metro Palace passage. It didn't make sense, but having gone along the passage, she continued past the Teddy Bears pub and the Police Headquarters along Na Perštýně Street, although she could have turned into it straight off National Avenue. From Na Perštýně Street she turned down St Bartholomew's Lane (Bartolomějská) and thence into the narrow, almost ravine-like College Lane (Konviktská), which runs between St Bartholomew's Lane and Bethlehem (Betlémské) Square.

The pram wheels squeaked on the uneven paving, the rear

left one threatening to drop off at any moment. By Bethlehem Chapel the old lady paused, tried to smooth out the rags in the pram. As before, the face of her doll – actually the Bambino di Praga – wasn't visible. I expect she was afraid someone might try to bewitch it. I once had a little black doll. I loved my little black doll most of all my dolls, though with time it lost its legs and at points where its black face was worn you could see pink. One day, at our house, a distant cousin of mine was playing with the little black doll and secretly abducted it. I remember going with my mother somewhere to the far side of Prague. My cousin handed it back in tears. But something had happened to it during those few hours. I didn't love it as much as before and in the end I let my mother throw it away broken.

She turned into Lily Lane (Liliová). I was still following her as if enchanted. For the first time in my life I noticed the sign on one of the houses – a hand with a walnut (isn't the walnut a symbol of virginity?). Then she turned off into Charles Street (Karlova). Ahead of me the house of the Golden Well rose in all its glory. Its façade is adorned with an entire gallery of statues, among them St Wenceslas and St John Nepomucene and one floor up Sts Sebastian and Roch, who afford protection from the plague. I thought I caught the crazed woman glancing up to where, in a recess-cave, some female saint rests.

At that moment, three students, shrieking happily, came rushing out of the Faculty of Theatre. They noticed the crazy woman and the Infant Jesus at once. They didn't seem surprised, in all likelihood they knew her by sight, she probably passes this way every day. And it possibly wasn't the first time they had put on their little dumb-show, which I witnessed. They doubled their backs like the old lady and pushed invisible prams before them, bouncing over the cobbles. It wasn't obvious whether the crazy woman was taking in their game or not. She drove on, obedient to her inner voice. And I walked on a few paces behind her. A few dozen yards on the girls lost interest in the game, waved to the crazy woman one last time and let her be.

The street made a few angular turns, but the old lady, without looking up, followed its course with absolute assurance. We came out into Little Square (Malé náměstí) and carried on from there to Old Town Square. She drove in among a crowd of foreigners waiting heads bent back in front of the astronomical clock, waiting for the show to begin. Just as the throng reluctantly parted to let her through, the hour struck, the little windows on the clock opened, and the apostles, one after another... Some of the onlookers weren't looking up though, but gazing mesmerised into the pram, possibly having spotted the Bambino di Praga, some may even have registered the unbelievable likeness to the statuette they had seen in a certain church.

They really may have seen the Bambino di Praga. I saw it again myself. Now I was walking close behind the crazy woman. As the pram leaned more and more to the left, the rags slipped off the dusky-olive face of the baby. It was looking towards the site of the executions. In its hand it clutched a shrivelled apple.

Then we drove along Celetná Street. Drove? She drove her pram, but I caught myself also pushing a pram in my mind (with the little black doll of my childhood?) and my back was slightly bent. She stopped at the corner of Celetná Street and Fruit Market (Ovocný trh). She raised her head, this time there was no mistaking the motion. Finally I understood. High on the angle of the Baroque house, rebuilt in the Cubist style by Gočar, there is a statue behind bars – the Black Madonna. The Black Mother of God holds a black Baby Jesus on her arm. The old lady held her gaze a long time. The infant looked steadily somewhere to one side. Then the crazy woman bent down to her pram. Only now did she notice that the baby was uncovered, and she wrapped it in the rags. She set off. She headed towards National Avenue, perhaps to the Platýz passage, from where again... How many more times would she describe her circular pilgrimage. I didn't follow her any further.

I must go back to Golden Lane once more. I am mystified that my journey below ground had ended at precisely that spot. Perhaps it meant something. Again I went through all my notes, jottings from books on the history of the lane. The little houses had originally been home to twenty-four Red Fusiliers, guardians of the ramparts, who had erected them here under the arches of a prison corridor. Allegedly, no alchemists, jewellers or goldsmiths ever did live here (so what about Professor Uhle?), that was just a legend derived from its name, which had originally been Goldsmiths' Lane (though why?). Again I read about Franz Kafka, Professor Uhle, Madame de Thèbes. Finally I came upon a short note, with no indication of its source. According to legend, the House of the Last Lamp stands here in Golden Lane. However, it can only be seen on certain nights; it encloses the hidden threshold between the visible and the invisible. I remembered that the hero of Meyrink's *Golem* had looked for it. In the final scene he finds it. On the walls of its garden there are frescoes illustrating the cult of Osiris – the deity that dies and revives – and its gate is surmounted by a hermaphrodite with a hare's head. Beyond the gate he spots his doppelganger, Athanasias Pernath, to whom he has come to return his hat. He does not cross the threshold.

The book on house signs does not record the House of the Last Lamp (but has its name anything to do with its sign?). The list knows only the House of the Private Lamp, but that is in Staré Město, in Revolution (Revoluční), previously Elizabeth (Eliščina) Avenue. And what if the circumstance that the house appears only on certain nights indicates some possible connection with the configuration of the planets and the phases of the Moon? I recalled one similar instance, mentioned by Chadraba in a book devoted to the symbolism of the Old Town bridge tower. He says that the tower of St Vitus' Cathedral and this tower are constructed in such a way that at the summer solstice, if we look from the axis of the bridge tower, the rays of the sun pass straight through the lantern in the tower of St Vitus' directly above the St Wenceslas Chapel, where the royal crown sits on the saint's head. Chadraba explains this by the fact that the bridge tower, like the Cathedral, is dedicated to St Vitus, who is the patron saint of the solstice. But that is not the end of the light-based mystery of the tower. On a ledge on its eastern façade there is a two-tailed lion, which seems to be looking down, as if enamoured, on the emblem of the fiery St Wenceslas eagle, located in the triangle above a blind circular arcade. According to Chadraba, this is a game being played with escutcheons, in connection with the Bohemian astrological prediction of Abbot Joachim, his prophecy about the last ruler who would come from Bohemia to capture Rome, subjugate the Pope, convert the pagans, conquer Jerusalem. One detail here – the addition of fiery tongues (of the Holy Spirit) to the Saint Wenceslas eagle – means rebirth and salvation through the monarchy. Chadraba maintains that this scene corresponds in a way to the invocation that was once inscribed on the gates of Rome and which we can still see on the Nové Město town-hall tower, the period counterpart to the Old Town bridge tower.

SIGNA TE, SIGNA, TEMERE ME TANGIS ET ANGIS
ROMA, TIBI SUBITO MOTIBUS IBIT AMOR

These lines, which read the same backwards as forwards, mean: *Reveal thyself as a sign (in the sky), in vain dost thou touch me and long for me, Rome, through the movements (of the stars) love will suddenly come to thee.* This is evidently a dialogue between the lion and the eagle in the prophetic sense mentioned above. Chadraba pursues his idea further. The lion emblematises the sun. St Vitus' Day is 15th June, which at the time was the date of the summer solstice. On that day, at high noon, the shadow of the lion touches the tip of the eagle and the whole group of statues on the façade is radiant in the sunlight. In the spirit of the myth of the Sun King, Chadraba then explains the other symbolic elements of the tower, in particular the pair of Charles IV (the old sun) and

Wenceslas (the new sun), above whom two fiery, rotating suns float like banners.

But what moment should I choose in order to touch the invisible house in Golden Lane (gold – the Sun?), cross its threshold and enter the sphere of the invisible? I would have to return to the lane time and again, pass its length countless times, by day and by night, until perhaps the moment would arrive one day and through the movements (of the stars) love would suddenly come to me. However, I lack the endurance, or maybe I'm not yet mad enough. And what if the old lady with her Infant Jesus is also describing some ritual circuit so that she might one day witness a miracle? Hence her repetitive circumambulation with her pram. She believes it will happen one day: the child will push aside the cloth from its dusky-olive face and wave to the knot of curious onlookers. In its other hand it will hold an unspoilt red apple.

FABRIC

A strong wind is blowing from the river, I can feel it at my back. It carries me up Kapr Street from the erstwhile ford towards *Old Jewry*, as this place was called at the end of the nineteenth century before the ghetto was redeveloped. I do not look back at the famous panorama. I have no doubt that the backdrop is where it should be.

It has occurred to me to pop into Broad Street, to the house where Jan E. had once shown me the shem, or rather *mezuzah*. I recognise the house at once, on that previous occasion I hadn't realised that it stood right next to the Jewish Cemetery. What novels will be written one day, in adulthood, by the children who are growing up in its rooms, whose windows give onto this cemetery? The mezuzah is in place. I touch it quivering in anticipation. At that moment I remember Hana Kalman, how I touched her forehead with my handkerchief and she came to life on the floor of the Theatre Cabinet. I also remembered her Sabbath skirt.

I wander the streets where once was the ghetto. I don't even know how I found myself by the Old-New Synagogue at the end of Maisel Street. I feel like an interloper. I make my way through the throng of people with Semitic eyes streaming between the synagogue and the cemetery. When the Jewish Quarter comes to life one day, and that day is surely not far off, there will be no admittance for goyim. An old man in a black hat passes me, he has a black velvet ribbon round his forehead. He strikes me as familiar. Deep in conversation with another Jew, he utters the name Daniel Mayer, his tone is highly excited. Three little girls come running in my direction, I have to step aside for them, off the pavement onto the roadway, they too have ribbons round their foreheads.

I'm actually walking through the Jewish Quarter hoping to find a fabric – fabric for the cover of this book. I pass along Joachim Street (Jáchymova). Although it leads from Paris Avenue quite close to Old Town Square, I think I am here for the first time. JEWISH MUSEUM. "I'm looking for a fabric," I explain to the concierge. She looks up, distrustful, from her knitting – a weird sister in a Jewish mould. After some time she does eventually open the lattice shutter and lets me in.

A woman in trousers gets up from a table, coming towards me. "Hana Kalman!" She shakes her head. Her name is Anna Holman. No, she'd never taken an exam in puppet theatre (she laughs at the idea), she had studied ethnography. So it probably really isn't her, when she comes up closer and half turns so that the sunlight falls on her face, she no longer resembles the student who had been carried off by the water king (someone or other told me that Dr B. left home one day never to return). She is like her, but only about as much as the name Anna Holman is like the name Hana Kalman.

Dr Holman opens out one Torah Ark curtain after another. "And you don't have three sisters – Fegal, Hyndl and Plumel?" She smiles: "Those aren't names any more, did you see them in a book somewhere?" And then my eye falls on one particular *parokhet*, it has a Hebrew inscription at the top, the middle is of blue satin with silver embroidering, the purple hem is also embroidered in silver. "Prague 1705," she says. I know where I've seen this curtain, certainly not so radiant, but then Dr Holman says it has recently been restored. My mind is made up, I'll use this one. "That's a good choice," says the woman who resembles Hana Kalman. She seems perfectly at ease.

Now the wind is in my face, thrusting me back to *Old Jewry*. Now I can sense the fragrance, or rather smell, of the river. The backdrop of Hradčany, lightly veiled in mist, appears where I expect it to. I reach the river. The water is murky like that time in my dream.

AFTER THE CELEBRATION

I was back at the Castle, wandering through its corridors and chambers. They were through with the celebration which, as in the distant past, had been taking place in the Spanish Hall, whose windows give on the Deer Fosse (the second tier of windows are mirrors – *trompe-l'œil*). But it was obvious that this hadn't been that New Year's celebration, it was still autumn, before long a year would have passed since revolution broke out in the City. The mortal remains of President Novotný, for whom, in the early 1960s, Young Pioneers put on a tableau about the generation that had sprung up, have been resting for many years now in one of Prague's cemeteries. From time to time I encounter guests from the celebration, they are wandering about the Castle much as I am.

"Everything ends, nothing begins." Where have I heard that before? Someone quietly beats a drum. I turn. Have they too been playing at the celebration? And what have I been playing? The one who plays Everyone is with them, I hope he isn't contemplating jumping into the Deer Fosse… But then, that time at Karlov, it was also only a game. "Everyone and Everything now stride towards Nothing." They speak their parts as if they were talking in their sleep. The golden bra of the lady playing Everything glints in the half-dark. "That ending signifies doubtless that Dame Fortune is our mistress ..." Nowhere do I see the wheel with its tarot cards, perhaps it is still hanging in the Spanish Hall. Nothing in its black cape passes close by me in the doorway, a white mask on its face. Only now do I see that in its gape a perfect set of silver teeth is bared.

I set off another way. I wouldn't want to go the way of Nothing, would I? For a moment I can still hear quiet drumming, a flute has just let out a feeble toot.

I seem to have ended in an abandoned wing. There are no carpets and the corridor is only dimly lit by a bulb hanging by a wire from the ceiling. It also dawns on me that for quite some time I haven't actually met anyone. I am so far away that not even the murmur of guests talking reaches me, and anyway the celebrations are more desultory than jubilant. On the other hand, I do catch a different sound. It seems familiar, but I can't put my finger on when or where I've heard it before.

The corridor narrows and seems to be rising gently. And everywhere there's that noise, now louder, now feebler. Suddenly it is broken by a shout. And then I remember. It's the sound that I've been hearing daily for some time now as I walk past the bus with videogames parked near the church wall. Gipsy teenagers hang about outside the bus. Once I noticed that the sound – the bubbling and whirring of the spheres – bounces back off the church wall. And that shout? Do they play these games up here at the Castle too, and has some youth just hit the target? I lay a hand on the door-handle, I want to establish whether they do play the same games here as in our square, perhaps the Castle Guards while away the time with them when they're off duty. It really does look as if I'm in some abandoned wing of the Castle, closed to visitors even during celebrations; all the rooms are locked.

I was just thinking of setting off back but sense that I won't find the way, I hadn't let a red thread out behind me, nor do I have with me a miraculous *Ainkhürn* horn, so probably my best option is to keep on going, to the centre of this labyrinth, if it has a centre. Eventually, one door-handle yields to my touch. My first idea is that I could be in the council room from whose window the Estates hurled Slavata and Martinic in 1618 (everyone survived that particular defenestration as if by some miracle – or as if in a game? – and the clerk, Fabricius, whom they also ejected, subsequently hurried off to Vienna; for his betrayal he earned the aristocratic agnomen of von Hohenfall), but I reject the notion at once. After all, the council room is quite near the Wenceslas Hall, it is still shown to visitors to the Castle. But this room is neglected and totally empty. What's that in the corner? Oh, it's a sunken pool, with a number of steps down into it. Someone has smashed up the tiles that once lined it, its bottom is strewn with rubbish, old papers.

Suddenly I see him. In the opposite corner. In the dim greenish light drifting from a screen on which some objects keep popping up and exploding – at this distance I can't tell what they are; glinting on the head of a man sitting in an armchair with his back to the pool I see – no, not a crown – a shock of ginger hair. The immobile face, which I am observing in profile, reflects fatigue, possibly profound grief. Was it he I'd heard shout out a moment before? As I approach he starts and looks up. It is the look of a harried animal. Maybe he's remembered me from today's celebration. What was it I had played? He gives me a twitchy smile out of the corner of his mouth. Then he returns to stare at the screen.

I leave on tiptoes so as not to disturb him, out into the corridor. I walk on. The bubbling and whirring of the spheres still reaches me from the devastated castle bathroom. Then there's another shout. Of winner or loser? What ceremony has been going on at the Castle today? What *tableau vivant* has been played out?

I catch the sound of an organ playing. I must be somewhere close by St Vitus' Cathedral. If I were to take the heavy handle of the door I'm looking at now and the handle gave, I might find myself in the royal oratory, overgrown with lush stone vegetation in the manner of the late Gothic Decorated style. Or might I have mounted a miniature pulpit? Or might I find myself in George of

Poděbrady Square, with the sound of the organ merging with the whirring of the spheres as on that earlier occasion? But I don't want to enter the church or go back home. For a moment more I remain in proximity to the man who is engaged in star wars in the one-time castle bathroom.

ANY TIME NOW…

For a long time now I've been uneasily observing some water jetting into the underpass at the Museum metro station. At first it was barely noticeable, it formed a rusty trickle. This dry summer the source dried up completely. Now it's autumn and it has sprung with renewed strength. It wends its way through the underground passage and disappears into cracks somewhere. Disappears? What is that strange gurgling and bubbling that can be heard two stations further down the line, at George of Poděbrady Square? The water is rising… In time it will flood the Prague Basin, rise to the Olšany Cemeteries and lap at the house of my childhood. Everything ends, Nothing begins.

There have been other disturbing signs. Do they have something to do with the special character of this City, which sprang up long ago almost as a feature of the natural landscape? That character survives in Staré Město, where streets suddenly narrow and change into little ravines, abutting end-to-end or at sharp angles to other streets, full of sudden turns. Here and there three-dimensional reliefs, statues and piers leap out of frontages and corners like saxicolous fungi. This peculiar growth principle, this exuberance that ceased many centuries ago, seems to have broken out anew in recent months. On a house at Můstek I have seen the head of a unicorn, thrusting its way to the surface through the new building, its horn having already broken through the masonry. A little further on, on National Avenue, a stone head is beginning to project from a wall, it once adorned a now demolished building. And in addition to signs from the past, encrusted on the new age, new signs are appearing all over the City. At the corner of Huss Street and Charles Street, on the route followed by the madwoman with her pram, a maiden has appeared on a spanking new jeweller's shop. Her likeness seems to combine the image of Melusina – the mermaid in an alchemist's manuscript – and a girl from one of Mucha's Art-Nouveau advertising posters. I am tempted to touch it each time I pass, run my hand over her perfectly smooth body. Let's hope no one takes a knife to it, out of curiosity splitting her wooden belly open by Caesarean section; overnight the jeweller's maiden would become a martyr. (I was passing that way again the other day and was horrified – instead of the maiden I saw there a whore. What had they done to her?)

I walk on. I sense that if I looked up now I would see that it isn't Mánes' astronomical clock on the Town Hall, or rather a copy of it (after all, the original is in the Municipal Museum), but that it's the Wheel of Fortune with tarot cards hanging up there. No one has spotted the switch yet, they're all looking up into the little windows and at Death. I turn into Iron Lane. I change my mind at once and am about to go back, but it's too late. A large, gaunt dog, my guide to the underworld, rubs against my leg and runs on. Perhaps I should follow him again, but I don't. I glance into the window of the Orient Café and in the glass see, horrified, my aged, crazed face.

I have heard that by order of the Abbot they are soon to remove the Bohemian lion from the courtyard at Strahov; in its place they intend to erect a column. A plague column? The papers report that the Communists have removed the urn with President Gottwald's ashes from the Liberation Memorial on Vítkov Hill and stored it in a safe place. Finally Everything is coming to Nothing…

The City has become host to dozens of prophets and healers, they make their prophecies and perform their miracles in the Hall of Sport, not far from Marold's panorama of the Battle of Lipany. One of them has declared there is a conspiracy that is spreading leaflets urging people to chant false mantras – MRM – their souls will be doomed. Could we suddenly be in Eco's *Foucault's*

Pendulum? On the back end of the bus with videogames, which seems to have dropped anchor by the church on the square for all eternity, the portrait of Václav Havel is no longer, all that remains is the inscription JESUS. If I take a few steps towards the post-box by the school, I will see a brand-new inscription on it – HAVEL = IDIOT. Like the annual ritual among primitive tribes – the old king has been killed and a new one will be crowned. He is still ensconced in the Castle, listening to the bubbling and whirring of the spheres, but any time now…

Who's tempting fate here? The blind youth? People step out of the blind youth's way, they avoid looking at his face, his eye-sockets are deformed. The blind youth walks through the gap in the crowd that is gathering by the Huss monument and muttering. Will the pyre not blaze up again soon? The man who played dead on 17 November has allegedly been identified. When he fell under a blow from a truncheon, they quickly wrapped him in a sheet and carried him away. It was seen by Drahomíra Dražská, in the dead man she recognised Martin Šmíd, it was all a put-up job. She knew it was secret agent Zifčák, first he'd played the part of the student Růžička, who led the procession into the trap on National Avenue, and then the part of the deceased Martin Šmíd. People! Our revolution was just a game, a conspiracy of the mighty, we've been chanting false mantras, our souls will be doomed… Was it really the blind youth that said that? No, he is walking through the crowd in silence towards Celetná Street.

The crowd is muttering. Many contemplate heading for the Castle, there could be another defenestration. This time the one to be tossed into the Castle ditch would be – no, they wouldn't find the President – Prince Schwarzenberg, followed by the press spokesman, Žantovský. At that moment you would hear, coming from St Vitus' Cathedral, the quiet weeping of the saint who, in his ducal helmet and with the sovereign's sword at his belt, would weep at the dissensions and troubles of this land. And in the Jewish Quarter, which is coming back out of its hundred-year sleep, shouting children would rub out the first letter of the word

EMET, someone has written it in chalk on the wall of the Old-New Synagogue, and the word that means *truth* would at once become MET, the word that means *death*. By then they would have found, at the Jewish Museum, that Dr Anna Holman was missing, once more she would have been carried off by the water king, she would not have been hiding behind someone else's name. And at the Castle Steps, the ones that had recently brought me to St Nicholas', a child's pram would come hurtling down (just as in Eisenstein's *The Battleship Potemkin*). And the Bambino di Praga? How had the madwoman come this far? MET. But all this, ladies and gentlemen, is just a play, at the end the dead will come to life and step up to the forestage (like on the ramp of the National Museum) and utter the carefully rehearsed sentence: "We are humb…" No! They will take a bow smiling sheepishly, the audience must forgive them, the memorial is off. From their mouths an inarticulate sound will issue, a dull muttering suggesting… Enough!

When I found myself in the depths of despair at the end of the performance, I saw those two again – the old man and the boy – it's now clear they are together. Only now have I noticed how strikingly alike they are, at least to the extent that the past can look like the future or the future like the past. It was on Wenceslas Square, next to the Blaník cinema. The boy was pointing somewhere towards the Museum. They were laughing at the boy's silly idea that a whale skeleton might swim out of the Museum onto the Square.

EPILOGUE

City of torment! City of puppets! You Monster! In all likelihood I am partly to blame for your awakening, I have brought you to life with words. In vain I now seek your tongue so that I can remove the shem concealed beneath it. In vain I touch you. I enter your gates, most of which these days go from nowhere to nowhere, I visit the deserted places of your memory, I read and write novels about you. I have been through ordeals by fire, air, earth and water (was that the right order?), but I know not whether I have become enlightened. You slip away from me as that fiery eagle evades the lion on the Old Town bridge tower. And yet I hope, City, that just as the lion's shadow touches the eagle for a brief moment once a year, so I too, for a brief moment, with a single word, will touch you, Beast of a City, as I perceived you in my early childhood. By that word I will lift the magical shem from you. And then once more you will drop back into sleep. Until...

Autumn 1990

Also available from Jantar Publishing

A KINGDOM OF SOULS
by Daniela Hodrová

Translation by Véronique Firkusny and Elena Sokol
Introduction by Elena Sokol

Through playful poetic prose, imaginatively blending
historical and cultural motifs with autobiographical moments,
Daniela Hodrová shares her unique perception of Prague.
A Kingdom of Souls is the first volume of this author's literary
journey — an unusual quest for self, for one's place in life and
in the world, a world that for Hodrová is embodied in Prague.

KYTICE
CZECH & ENGLISH BILINGUAL EDITION
by Karel Jaromír Erben

Translation and Introduction by Susan Reynolds

Kytice was inspired by Erben's love of Slavonic myth and
the folklore surrounding such creatures as the Noonday
Witch and the Water Goblin. First published in 1853,
these poems, along with Mácha's *Máj* and Němcová's
Babička, are the best loved and most widely read 19th
century Czech classics. Published in the expanded 1861
version, the collection has moved generations of artists
and composers, including Dvořák, Smetana and Janáček.

www.jantarpublishing.com

Olšany cemetery

Wenceslas Square (nr Nat museum)
. Slavs armor (→ Prague Castle)
. Libuše's prophesy - like a great city